Stepping Stone

WALTER MOSLEY

CROSSTOWN TO OBLIVION

Stepping Stone

TOR®

A TOM DOHERTY ASSOCIATES BOOK • NEW YORK

This is a work of fiction. All of the characters, organizations, and events portrayed in these novellas are either products of the author's imagination or are used fictitiously.

STEPPING STONE / LOVE MACHINE

Copyright © 2013 by Walter Mosley

All rights reserved.

Illustrations by Greg Ruth

A Tor Book
Published by Tom Doherty Associates, LLC
175 Fifth Avenue
New York, NY 10010

www.tor-forge.com

Tor® is a registered trademark of Tom Doherty Associates, LLC.

Library of Congress Cataloging-in-Publication Data

Mosley, Walter.
　　Stepping stone ; Love machine / Walter Mosley.—First edition.
　　　　p. cm.—(Crosstown to oblivion)
　　ISBN 978-0-7653-3010-9 (hardcover)
　　ISBN 978-1-4299-4311-6 (e-book)
　　I. Mosley, Walter. Stepping stone.　II. Mosley, Walter. Love machine.　III. Title.　IV. Title: Love machine.
　　PS3563.O88456S74 2013
　　813'.54—dc23

2012042628

Tor books may be purchased for educational, business, or promotional use. For information on bulk purchases, please contact Macmillan Corporate and Premium Sales Department at 1-800-221-7945 extension 5442 or write specialmarkets@macmillan.com.

First Edition: April 2013

Printed in the United States of America

0　9　8　7　6　5　4　3　2　1

For Julia Masnik,
who makes the impossible
possible

ACKNOWLEDGMENTS

In memory of Jayne Cortez.

PART ONE

"EXCUSE ME," a young woman said from behind.

The elevator car was stopped at the nineteenth floor of the Westerly Building and my mail cart was blocking her exit. But the thing was I didn't notice her standing there behind me and when I had gotten in, the elevator car had been empty, I was sure of that.

I had worked for Higgenbothem, Brightend, and Hoad for twenty-one years with nothing out of the ordinary happening. I mean, there was the World Trade Center disaster down around Wall Street and some freakish weather now and again; we, the nation, were fighting a war against somebody, and preparing to fight against somebody else, in the Middle East, though no one seemed to be quite sure who the enemy actually was. There were economic reversals and the rent, for most New Yorkers, had gone through the up- stairs neighbor's roof but nothing unusual had happened within the confines of HBH proper.

My employer occupied floors sixteen to twenty-two in the Westerly Building on East Fifty-sixth Street. I worked in the mailroom, had done so since my first day on the job in 1986. I started out as a mail delivery clerk and had ended up the manager of the department. There were just three employees in my section. The only difference between me and my two perpetually temporary subordinates was a title and $4.65 an hour. Kala Daws and Pete Mulray were responsible for floors sixteen to twenty-one, whereas I only had to deliver mail on the top floor and do the managerial paperwork for our small section, that was once a hallway, on floor seventeen.

I never was sure exactly what HBH did. It had something to do with finance and there were executives from around the globe that spent as much as twenty-four hours a day studying graphs and documents in foreign languages on their huge plasma screens. I didn't even know the names of most of the languages nor did I understand the significance of the charts. But that wasn't unusual. I had, what they called at my uptown high school, a learning disability. Information made it into my mind but unless it had some direct relation to the way I saw the world I wasn't normally capable of using it. And the way I saw things had very little in common with my teachers, at least most of them.

"That don't sound like no disability to me," my aunt Tiny used to say when my counselors called. "Sounds more like common sense."

Earlier on I had problems with what my teachers termed as "communication skills." I couldn't speak clearly and often used words in the wrong order when under pressure or confused. I could write okay and I had been reading voraciously since the age of six. I didn't have trouble putting words down on, or picking them up from, paper but people didn't want to read the notes of a boy who had a perfectly good voice and most of my teachers didn't believe I was really reading the books that I carried everywhere.

My fourth-grade teacher, Miss Boucher, used to keep me

after school and worked to help me think about how I put my words together. We would sit for hours in the study room of the library and talk. Whenever I made a mistake she would look at me and touch my hand. I'd realize what I had done wrong and repeat the phrase correctly. By the sixth grade I rarely misspoke anymore.

Miss Boucher cured my *disability* but I was already tagged as a slow learner and mildly retarded so I was shunted down a particular path of learning that was inapplicable to my needs but still valid, in a way—because all my teachers, except Miss Boucher, believed that I couldn't be taught.

I wasn't bothered much by what people thought, however. School didn't interest me very much and I spent most of the time considering simple things like ants and cloud formations; the way brides smile on their wedding days and all the possible patterns that water can make if you turn on the faucet quickly and then slam it shut. Sometimes I'd sit all day in my small eastside apartment watching the various arrangements of people as they walked down the street.

THE YEAR BEFORE that girl appeared behind me on the elevator I went back to my old elementary school and asked if Miss Boucher still taught there. It was a long shot but I remembered she was young when I was in her class and I had just that March reached the age of forty.

"And who's asking?" the head of the office inquired.

"My name is Truman Pope," I said. "I used to go to school here and Miss Boucher taught me to get my words right."

The registrar, Nancy Bendheim, had a stern visage and a reluctant air about her. But when I explained how Miss Boucher had impacted my life she smiled a real smile and nodded.

"Alana still teaches here," the registrar told me. "She's in class right now but she'll be finished at eleven thirty. If you'd like to wait . . ."

Mrs. Bendheim let me sit in a parent-teacher conference room down the hall from her office. The room was quite small with a beat-up old class table for a desk and two chairs. It was a grim place with light green, stained walls and a pitted wooden floor. But there was a window that looked out into the branches of an oak tree. The lunch courtyard was on a lower level than the entrance of the school and so the room was one floor up. There were all kinds of activities going on among the branches. Spring leaves, that youthful kind of green, and insects, caterpillars, sparrows, starlings, and even one frisky gray squirrel. There were initials carved here and there by brave student climbers and a pair of tennis shoes that had the laces tied together hanging from a precarious branch that was, no doubt, too perilous a place for the custodial staff to reach.

Those shoes caught my attention. They were old and weathered, had probably been hanging there for a few years. I imagined the boy who, after having outgrown his old footwear, wanted to get one more bit of use out of them. I thought of how happy he must have been when the bolo he threw grabbed on to that skinny branch. Did he pass by below every day in the lunch court and look up to see his finest hour?

"Truman?" a gentle voice said.

Turning away from the window I saw her through a small boy's eyes. She was still slender, still copper skinned with brown eyes. Her brown hair had become mostly gray but that was the only difference. Judging from her face she had not aged a day since the afternoon I had said, "I watch go him," and she touched the back of my hand so lightly that it almost tickled.

"Is that really you?" she asked, a friendly smile brightening the dull room.

"Um," I said, unable to keep from grinning myself. "I, uh, I came by because I had the day off and I was walking around the old neighborhood and remembered, I mean thought about you."

Miss Boucher moved to the chair next to my station at the window and sat so gracefully that I experienced a sudden intake of breath as I used to when I had my schoolboy crush on her.

"How are you doing, Truman?"

"I was just walking around the old neighborhood . . ."

She touched my hand to get me beyond the skip in the scratched record of my mind.

"I wanted to see if you were still here to ask you something," I said.

"What's that?" she asked.

I remember looking into her eyes amazed that more than thirty years had elapsed.

"I don't know," I said. "I mean I guess it was just to say thank you. You know you were the only teacher I ever had who didn't think I was an idiot. I mean . . . They always said that I had a learning disorder but, but . . ."

"But that's just because they couldn't understand you," the older but still lovely teacher said, finishing my words now because there was no more I had to learn.

"Yeah, I guess."

"So you just came by to say thank you?" she asked me.

"Didn't you always used to say to me that if there was something then there was always something else?" I asked.

Miss Boucher smiled.

"Yeah, so," I blundered on, "I guess I came here because I wanted to see you again and to thank you for helping me be okay with things."

"What things?" she asked.

Answering that one question I must have rambled on for half an hour. I told her about how I had been labeled overactive by school officials and how I could never go to college. I couldn't have gone anyway because my aunt Tiny got sick when I graduated high school and I had to work to help her until she was old enough for the state to foot the bill. I talked about my job and how much I liked moving from station to station delivering mail to people who rarely realized that I was even there.

". . . and, anyway, I was, I just wanted to say thanks. You know most of my teachers never liked me. Or maybe not, I mean they didn't not like me it's just that they didn't care and they didn't understand. I mean I don't think that it was because I'm black or anything. Tish Loman and Ronnie Dewar got along with some of the same teachers in different classes and they didn't have any problems. But it was just that nobody would ever listen. I tried, I tried to do how you taught me but . . .

"Anyway. I'm not complaining, it's just that I always think about how nice you were and how the reason I can do my job and make it to manager is because you showed me how to see things and say them too. I mean, there's nothing wrong with me—"

"Certainly not," Alana Boucher agreed.

There we were, in that ugly room sitting on the wrong side of the window, next to the branches of an ancient oak. Miss Boucher put her hand on mine as she had done so many years before.

"So you're still here," I said to fill in the silence.

"Where else would I be?" she said.

"If you taught all the classes in this school I wouldn't have been called stupid by anybody and I could have gone to college," I said.

"And what would you have done then?" she asked, smiling, holding my hand.

"I could have been one of those guys in suits making good money. My aunt Tiny wouldn't be in a rest home but in a good place or in her own home with a nurse to make sure she takes her meds . . ." I wanted to say more but if I kept talking I would have started crying.

"I bet you visit your auntie every week," Miss Boucher said.

I did see Aunt Tiny on Tuesdays, Thursdays, and most Saturdays. But nobody knew that. I remembered then that Miss Boucher seemed to know what I was thinking and what I was doing without me having to say. It was like she could see into my mind.

"And those people who work in those offices don't know

birdcalls and how clouds spin," she continued. "They don't know how to sit down and watch and listen so closely that the world seems to stop."

She said more but I stopped listening to the words and went into a kind of trance. As I sat there and looked out I could see three hundred and sixty degrees around me, more, because I could see above and below too. The three dimensions of space flattened out in front of me and I could see it all as if it was on a movie screen. There was no up or down, front or back.

I remembered then why I had missed Miss Boucher so much. Often when I was with her as a child I had the experience of *wide perception*. I could see a spider crawling on the wall behind me and feel the wind against the window outside. The world became larger and more intricate.

In that ugly green room I could feel the grin on my lips and energy thrumming from the boiler room three floors below. I could feel the sky even and, when everything inside me went still, I perceived glimmers of life outside in the hallway and down in the lunch yard.

I knew that it was just an illusion but it felt good . . . like everything.

"But," I said, coming out of the reverie, "but those guys at HBH are rich. Nobody wants to pay me to sit and watch bugs crawl."

"Maybe you aren't watching closely enough," Alana Boucher suggested.

I don't remember much after that. I sat forward in my chair to hear her better and she took my hand in both of hers. We talked, I'm sure of that, but I didn't remember a word of what we said until the end when we were standing outside on the sidewalk in front of the school.

"You have to pay very close attention, Truman," she was telling me. "The truth will reveal itself if you watch with intention."

"Why were you always so nice to me?" I asked her. The answer to that question was the real reason I had come.

For a moment she just stood there looking at something above my head.

"I loved spending time with you," she said at last. "The other teachers never understood how special you were. When we would sit in the remedial room and talk I began to feel elation and hope. You would show me things outside the window—birds and bulky little beetles trundling along. It was like you gave me a new pair of eyes."

I came there to thank my teacher but our last words were her expression of gratitude. I left her feeling mildly confused but happy, still and all.

That evening I went to visit Aunt Tiny at Eastside Nursing Home for the Elderly. She was in the ward on the fourth floor near a window that looked down on Eighty-third Street. I had moved to the eastside in order to be close to her.

Tiny weighed well over three hundred pounds and she was shorter even than I am.

The hippopotamus and the spider monkey, she used to say when I was small and she held me in her arms looking into the full-length plastic dressing mirror she had in her bedroom.

The world and her moon, I would respond, remembering a phrase from a children's book I'd once read.

"Hi, monkey," she said when I pulled up a stool next to her chair by the window.

"Hi, Aunt Tiny."

Tiny wasn't small and she wasn't old either. But at sixty-eight, with nearly twenty years of *retirement* already behind her, she had done forty years of hard labor and was, as she said, *just tired—body and soul.*

"What you do at work today, sugar?" she asked me.

The two things that Tiny and I had in common were our dark skin tones and the fact that we liked to sit and talk at the end of the day.

"I took the day off."

"You played hooky from work?" she asked with a mischievous smile on her broad mouth.

"I took a personal day and went to my old school to see Miss Boucher."

"She still walk there?"

"Uh-huh."

"How is that nice lady?" Tiny asked. She lived in a rest home not for her mind but simply because she was too tired even to walk more than a few paces on her own.

I told Tiny about our talk and when I was finished she said, "Remember, Baby, anything Miss Boucher says is important. Even if you don't understand, even if you don't remember exactly what she said, you keep them words in your heart because that woman know sumpin'."

And so a year had gone by and I watched everything that

happened around me. I watched walls and floors, the ceilings and the people who never noticed me. I sat in my one-room apartment and looked out of the window at the brick buildings across the street.

AND THEN, "Excuse me," a young woman said from behind my cart in the elevator car.

I pulled the mail cart out of the way. As she eased around I studied her. She had long, thick hair that was neither red nor brown but a color somewhere between the two. Her skin was ecru and her eyes were on the reddish side of violet. The pantsuit she wore was light yellow in color with intricate drab green designs etched here and there. The fabric was light, almost like pajamas and her shoes were burgundy and looked to be made from glass or at least a hard plastic.

"Sorry," I said.

She smiled and nodded, gliding out into the hallway. She had moved beyond my line of sight when I got the sudden urge to call out to her. I blocked the elevator doors with the cart and jumped out in the hall. No more than a few seconds had gone by but she was gone—vanished.

I was about to run down to the turn when someone shouted, "Hey, what's wrong with you? You think this is your own private elevator?"

This shocked me because I had thought I was in the elevator alone. But looking back into the car there were six people standing there; among them the senior VP Mr. Alan Travane and Lana Metcalf the vice president in charge of human resources.

After a moment's hesitation I jumped back into the elevator moving my cart to allow the doors to close.

Everyone got out on the next floor except Miss Metcalf. She was younger than I, short, my height, and very pale skinned.

"Please come to my office at four forty-five this afternoon, Mister . . . ?"

"Pope."

"Excuse me?" she asked as if she thought I were making a joke.

"Truman Pope is my name," I said still wondering about the strange-eyed girl.

"Do you know who I am?"

"Yes, Miss Metcalf."

"Then I'll see you at my office at four forty-five," she said as she got off.

The doors closed on her and I stood there wondering where that girl had gone.

"So what happened with you and Miss Metcalf?" Kala Daws asked me at the sorting table that noon. She, Pete, and I were having sandwiches for lunch as we did most days.

"Um," I said trying to conjure up the image of the events in the elevator. This was difficult because there were two superimposed memories: the sudden appearance of the girl in yellow and the angry riders whom I did not see until I turned back. There was something about the turning back that seemed most important.

"What's wrong, True?" Pete asked. "You havin' one'a your spells?"

The question brought me back to the table with my friends, still unable to recall the events in question with any clarity.

"I blocked the elevator door and . . . and there were people in a hurry behind me," I said.

"So why you do that?" Kala asked. She was young and cream brown, a graduate from Wesleyan waiting to be promoted.

She and Pete were both what the company called floaters. These were entry-level positions where, under the watchful eye of Miss Metcalf's assistant Stella Furman, potential executives were introduced to HBH by working in various operations areas.

Floaters almost always started in the mailroom. That way they moved around the entire company and began to see how things worked. Most floaters understood more about HBH in one month than I had gleaned in my twenty-one years on the job.

I was the only permanent employee in the mailroom.

"I thought I saw somebody," I said in answer to Kala's question.

"And so you blocked the door with your cart with two vice presidents and a manager in the car?" Pete asked.

Pete was a well-built young white guy. He'd graduated from Harvard and his father was on the board of HBH. He was affable and friendly and I thought that there might be something going on between him and Kala. I liked both of them. I never learned how to act my age (as my teachers so often told me) and so I usually got along well with young people.

"Yeah," I said lamely. "Yeah. I just blocked the door and went out and looked."

"Why, True?" Kala asked almost plaintively.

"I thought I was alone in the elevator. I guess I was in a kind of a daze."

"Don't say that to Lana when you go to her office," Pete said. He called all the VPs, managers, and even the owners, by their first names. "Just tell her that you thought you thought you saw somebody and acted out of impulse."

I smiled and nodded. It was nice that the kids wanted to help me. A few of the floaters who stayed at HBH smiled and said hi to me when I dropped off their mail. But, more often than not, the ones who passed through my mailroom resented the fact that I was their manager. Most times they tried to reorganize my system because they had college degrees and I was just a drudge.

But Kala was a young black woman who had been trained to respect her elders while Pete, on the other hand, was born of privilege and felt that it was beneath him to compete with the working classes.

We ate our sandwiches and the kids made suggestions as to what I should say in my disciplinary meeting with Lana Metcalf. Their words were like the pleasant chatter of frisky birds in a summer tree. I heard them and nodded now and again but the only thing on my mind was that girl in the yellow pj's walking in and out of my life in just a few seconds.

"COME IN," Lana Metcalf said in a stern yet evenly me-
tered voice. I had been waiting in the antechamber of her
office for twenty-six minutes.

I had never been inside the her office before because I'd
always left mail for her, and her predecessors, at the assistant's desk. It was a room both shallow and wide with
full-length windows that peeked around other skyscrapers,
offering a glimpse of the East River. Her desk had a green-
tinted glass top and there were no books, photographs,
knickknacks, or doodads anywhere in evidence. It was a
room with no character and a view, as Kala would say, to
die for.

"Have a seat, Mr. Pope."

I did as she asked and tried to keep my eyes on her face
so that the cityscape didn't distract me. I gave a wan smile
and waited for the hammer to drop.

"What was that in the elevator this morning?" she asked
without pleasantry.

She was a handsome woman. Some might have called her
pretty or at least attractive. But there was a hardness to
her face. She seemed to be hiding more than she showed. It
struck me at that moment that most people I met used up
the greater part of their resources, their personalities, hiding from the eyes of others. This was a kind of revelation
for me.

I spent most of my time thinking and watching. I had no
TV or computer. I didn't even own a radio. I read books at
bedtime, any book I happened to have at hand, and before
that I spent my time observing anything that moved or had
an interesting form. One night I spent more than an hour

examining the thick black cord plugged into the wall and connected to my toaster oven . . .

"Mr. Pope," Lana Metcalf said peevishly.

"Yes?"

"About this morning."

"I thought I saw someone in the hall," I said. "A woman in a yellow pantsuit. I thought I saw her drop something and went out to pick it up for her. I guess I was mistaken."

This was the story that Kala and Pete had suggested I use. Lana was studying me.

"Are you . . . under a doctor's care, Mr. Pope?"

"No."

"A mental health care professional?"

"No."

"Would you submit to a drug test?"

"Do I have to?" I asked.

This question stymied Miss Metcalf. HR had all kinds of rules and regulations that they had to follow. Her brows furrowed.

"No," she said after a moment more of scrutiny. "No, you don't. I can't force you to do so without three complaints on file."

"I've worked here for twenty-one years, ma'am," I said. "Nobody has ever had a complaint about me or my work . . . that I know of. I've never missed a day due to sickness and I don't take days off if there's no one trained in the mailroom."

"There are four reports that your mail delivery system is faulty," she said. She spoke with both anger and vindication in her tone.

"Has anyone ever complained that they haven't gotten their mail?"

Again she was stumped. This only served to stoke her anger.

"There wasn't anyone in the hall," she said.

These words stung me. As the day had progressed I had become obsessed with the girl in yellow. I was convinced that she was what Miss Boucher had told me to look for. But I was too late, too slow. Now I'd missed the most important moment in my life.

"I said that there wasn't anyone there," Metcalf was saying.

"Yes, ma'am. I know that now."

"So what possessed you to block the door and walk out into the hall?" she asked.

"I've answered that question already."

"And you refuse to take a drug test?"

"Do I have to take one?"

Scrutiny turned to resentment in her eyes. It was something like the sky when it slowly turns from a pale yellow to orange in some sunrises.

Metcalf reminded me of my teachers in school. She got angry when I said things that she couldn't refute. She expected me to be the fool from the mailroom, the man with the low IQ who managed to get a pity diploma from a substandard city high school. Neither my teachers, nor she, had any idea of what went on in my mind. But I had no way of letting her know. She would never listen to me. She could only get angry when I didn't submit the way she wanted me to.

"I'll be getting back to you, Mr. Pope," Metcalf said, after pausing to subdue her irritation.

Between two buildings at the end of the street I saw a hawk flash by. This sight elated me, made me forget the anger of the earthbound VP.

"I said that I'll get back to you," Metcalf told me.

"So I can go?"

"Yes. But this isn't over."

"What?"

"Excuse me?"

"What isn't over, Miss Metcalf? I mean I stopped the elevator because I thought I saw something. That's all. I didn't steal anything or insult someone. I just made a mistake. Why can't it be over?"

"I'll be getting back to you," she said again.

ON THE WALK home there were tears in my eyes. I was crying but not sobbing or bawling. It was a gentle sorrow passing through me, a feeling of loss, of a deficiency caused by the flash of yellow, like that hawk. I knew that I had missed something important that day and I wasn't sure the chance would ever come again.

Maybe I was retarded, as so many of my teachers had told Aunt Tiny; not stupid, but underdeveloped like a hard avocado. The kids in my schools became accountants and criminals, soldiers and whores; they either got jobs or went to prison but regardless of what they did it made sense in the world we lived in. I didn't make sense, not even to myself. I never knew my parents or had any family outside

of Aunt Tiny. I couldn't even talk right until Miss Boucher
with her gentle ways taught me how.

I was lacking in most things but I did have a telephone.
That was one thing that made me like other people. That
was one thing that made me normal.

The phone rang at 8:16 that evening. I wondered, on the
first ring, who it might be. I didn't have any friends outside
of Aunt Tiny and getting to the phone was a chore for her.
On the second ring I worried that it was the nursing home
calling to tell me that Tiny was sick or maybe dead.

"Hello?"

"True?"

"Oh . . . Hi, Olive."

"You don't sound happy to hear me," she said.

"No, it's not that," I said. "I was worried that it might be
the place where Aunt Tiny's staying. I thought that maybe
she was sick."

"Oh," Olive said.

OLIVE BREVE HAD been my girlfriend for a few months
twelve years before. She was the only woman that I'd ever
had sex with. We met in a small library in the West Village
where I used to go to read on Saturdays. We started talking
about ants. I was infatuated with the idea of pheromones as
a kind of communication. Olive asked me what I was reading and we started talking about smell in ants and even in
humans. Later on she told me she thought I was talking
about sex, that's why she asked me up to her apartment

when we'd had coffee together after the fourth time we talked.

Olive was a big woman when I met her, forty-five pounds overweight by her own underestimation. She also told me that she hadn't had a boyfriend in at least three years. When she found out that I'd never had a girlfriend (or sex) she had me take off my clothes and from that day for the next eighteen weeks and four days she gave me almost daily lessons in lovemaking. Olive worked at a small investment house down in Tribeca and I'd go there every day and walk with her to her place on the Upper West Side. I did this because she needed someone to help her with her diet and exercise regimen and I was besotted by the sex.

I thought there was something wrong with me and so I never really considered having a girlfriend or any kind of sexual relations. But once I got to know Olive I went crazy. We walked and ate salads together and had sex all the time.

I did whatever Olive asked me to do as long as it didn't get in the way of my job. I had to work hard because Tiny was already *retired* and needed my help.

Olive lost the weight and soon after met Tristram Charles. After fifteen weeks of walking Olive started jogging. I tried to do that with her but she was stronger than I and had a much better wind. She met Tristram on a jog in Central Park and was soon lost to me.

"HOW ARE YOU, Olive?" I asked sitting there in my solitary studio.

"Fine."

I was thinking that Aunt Tiny always told me that Olive would call one day.

Don't you worry, Baby, Tiny would say, *that white girl's gonna call. You just wait and see.*

"How's your husband?" I said when Olive was quiet.

"I was wondering if you wanted to get together for coffee one day," she replied.

"Um, sure. I guess."

"You don't know?" she asked, peevishly.

"We haven't talked at all in twelve years, Olive. I'm just a little surprised to hear from you, that's all."

"I'll tell you all about it at coffee, okay? . . . Day after tomorrow?"

We made a plan to meet at a chain coffee place across the street from her work on Thursday. I didn't really want to go but I rarely said no to anything that I didn't have a solid reason for. Olive and I had been friends as well as lovers—that's why I was so sad when she refused to see me while being courted by Tristram Charles.

THE NEXT MORNING went fine. There was a lot of interoffice mail to sort and Kala and Pete did a really good job keeping up. I liked it when I had to concentrate on the job in front of me. It kept me from drifting and staring off into space.

But at lunch I learned that Lana Metcalf had approached each of my deliverers on their routes and asked them about me.

"What did she want to know?"

"She asked both of us if you ever seemed drunk or high at work," Kala told me.

"And she wanted to know if you seemed odd," Pete added, "if you seemed unbalanced."

"What did you say?"

"She talked to me first," Kala said. "I told her that you were always proper and on top of the work, that you were never inappropriate or strange. Then I called Pete on his cell so that he wouldn't get blindsided."

"I told her the same thing, True," Pete said. "That woman wants to get you fired, man."

After Kala and Pete went off on their afternoon rounds I sat down at the sorting table and thought about the possibility of losing my job. I supposed that I could find work somewhere else. It seemed crazy to me that one mistake in twenty-one years could get me fired.

I must have worried about my predicament for quarter of an hour or so when I heard the buzzing. A big green housefly had somehow made it into the long corridor that had been made into the mailroom.

I loved it on those summer days when some wild, untamable creature like a fly would make its way from the outside world to my seventeenth-floor domain. Having it hum around the room added a kind of natural music to my day. I forgot about Lana Metcalf and unemployment. I did my job and made deep droning noises in my throat to accompany my newest friend.

———

AT 7:15 THE next morning an athletic man in a dark gray suit was waiting in the mailroom, seated at the sorting table.

"Mr. Pope?" the man asked rising from his chair.

"Yes?"

"My name's Harry Driscoll. I work for an outside company that audits the procedures of departments in corporations."

He handed me a letter on operations letterhead informing me that this *audit* was authorized by the VP in charge, an H. Michael Samson.

Driscoll shook my hand. He was younger than I, but not by much—tall and white. His smile was insincere, I remember that most.

"Do you always get in this early?" Driscoll asked me.

"Between seven and seven thirty."

"You're not due in till eight forty-five," he said, giving me that smile that was not a smile.

"I guess not."

"Do you find that you need extra hours to do your job?"

"Sometimes there's a lot of mail from the night before," I said. "People work all kinds of long hours here. So if there's a backlog I can jump on it. If not I have my coffee and ease into the day. I go to bed early and get up about five. I like the walk to work in the morning before the crowds are out."

Driscoll frowned and then nodded.

"Well," he said, "don't mind me. I'm just going to be sitting around observing. I may ask you a question now and then. You have two assistants, right?"

"Executive floaters," I said, "Kala and Pete. They get in around eight forty-five."

IT WAS ODD having a fourth person in the mailroom. There was more than enough space for him but he threw off the balance. Pete didn't like Harry; I could see that by the way the Harvard grad avoided him. Kala was actually rude.

"Who sent you?" she asked after he introduced himself.

"I work for Donner and Pride."

"Who hired them?" she asked.

"It was a corporate decision," he said.

"How do we even know that you should be here? Nobody called."

"I was sent by Mr. Samson from operations. Do you want to see the letter?" When he wasn't smiling Driscoll seemed a bit more honest.

I worried about Kala getting herself into trouble and was looking for a way to interrupt when the phone rang. Pete answered but both Harry and Kala were distracted by the call.

After he got off the line Pete said to me, "That was Stella Furman from HR. She wants the files on a man named Horace Trippman from 1993."

"What bullshit," Kala said.

"You guys better get on your rounds," I said, needing to separate Driscoll and Kala.

I suppose there was some authority in my voice because both kids gave me an odd stare. When they were off with their carts I went to my desk and unlocked the bottom drawer with a little copper key that had been on my key chain for seventeen years. From the drawer I retrieved another key chain.

"Where are you going?" Driscoll asked as I went toward the door.

"Getting a file for HR," I said.

"I'll come with you."

"No. You need a security clearance to go down into our onsite storage facility. The letter you have doesn't give you that clearance."

"But they told me I could go anywhere with you."

"They don't say that in the letter," I said.

Driscoll was about to say something else but I turned away and left.

THERE WAS A dedicated car at the far northwest end of the elevator bank. You also needed a special key to operate the call button. After a while I remembered which key and turned on the mechanism. I felt rushed. I didn't want Harry Driscoll following me down to the subbasement of the Westerly Building. It had been a long time since I was in storage and him looking over my shoulder would have made me nervous.

The car took a long time to get there but Driscoll didn't follow me so it turned out okay.

THAT ELEVATOR CAR was larger than the rest, designed to move furniture and filing cabinets. The walls were draped with canvas to protect them from damage in moving. I used my key to indicate the fifth-level subbasement and stood there facing the crack in the doors.

"Pardon me," a voice said.

My heart skipped. I didn't say a word and I didn't turn fearing that she would vanish if I did anything.

"Excuse me," she said.

I felt the hand on my shoulder but still I could not turn or speak.

"Truman."

I steeled myself and swiveled from the waist.

There she was—the ecru-colored flower child in her Oz-like ruby hued shoes.

"Hi," I said and she smiled. "I thought I made you up."

"No. I'm very real but not everyone can see me."

"Why not?"

"Because not everyone can see, really see. They make up the world that they know and then believe in things that aren't there at all."

"What's your name?" I asked.

She was an inch or so taller than I and so she had to lean over a bit in order to kiss me. It was a light meeting of our lips. There was small electrical shock but I didn't mind.

"I've been wanting to do that," she said. "People call me Minerva. And you are Truman Pope."

"I don't understand," I said. "How did you get here? Why didn't anybody but me see you? What's happening to me?"

"On High once told me that it's a question of harmonics," Minerva replied. "You aren't *seeing* me but rather you *hear* me, but not with your ears. There's a resonance that beings like you and I have in common. We also resonate with certain places."

Saying this she touched the center of my chest. I felt a thrumming there that reminded me of the fly in the mailroom.

The elevator doors came open then.

The storage floor was almost always empty and so it was usually dark. But when anyone walked out of the elevator a motion sensor turned the lights on.

Minerva giggled at the sudden brilliance.

Before us was a vast room with high ceilings and concrete-floored aisles that led down long rows of storage cages. Every office in the Westerly Building had at least one storage chamber; HBH had a whole room at the far end of the rightmost aisle.

"Are you real?" I asked Minerva as we walked. "Or am I going crazy?"

"I'm real," she said with conviction.

She walked with me down to the storage room door and waited patiently while I fumbled around trying to find the right key. We passed into the stale-smelling file space, banks of overhead lights snapping on as we did so.

"Do you want to make love to me, Truman Pope?" she asked when I closed the door.

"Um," I said.

She laughed and did a delicate and dancerly turn. The freedom in that simple movement caused a vacuum in my chest.

"Who are you?" I asked again.

"We," she said, "you and I are many different things. Offspring and parents, living and dying, climbers who descend, lovers that hate . . . Today I am a portent and you are the darkness finally yielding to the light."

"I don't understand."

"You haven't answered my question," she said.

"Here on the floor in the dust?" I asked.

Minerva laughed loudly but somehow the sounds were hushed as soon as they were heard. I think I was a little afraid of her right then.

"Are you afraid, Truman Pope?" This was odd because I had never been afraid of anything—ever.

"Only a little on the inside," I said.

"Of me?"

"No, not you," I said. "Of something that I've always felt but could never, never say."

"What's that, Truman Pope?"

"It's like my whole life I've had to live on a skinny ledge outside the window of a tall building way up above the street. Nobody knows I'm out there and they all have their windows locked and barred. I edge my way along afraid that I'll doze off and fall and so I hug the wall and keep on moving hoping for a place that's wide enough where I could sit and think."

The words came out of me as if I had given it a lot of thought but really I was more surprised by what I said than I was by the odd elfin girl-child.

"That's how everybody lives," she said. "Everybody in the Westerly Building and Midtown and the western hemisphere. People in Mongolia and China and Peru all hug that same wall. But here and today I am a door in the stone that keeps you out. I am the passageway to another side of you."

These words brought tears to my eyes. I had been waiting to hear someone say something like that my entire life but hadn't known it. I didn't know what to say so I went down the long aisle of dusty black metal filing cabinets searching for the Ts in 1993. I found Horace Trippman's file and sneezed from the dust. Minerva was behind me, standing very close. When I turned around we were face to face.

"I have to bring this file to Human Resources," I said.

"Why?"

"Because it's my job."

A grin spread across her wide, sensual mouth.

"Do you always do your job, True?"

"I guess."

"That's all we need from you."

She kissed me again, lightly, her mouth partly open. Backing away, I swallowed hard and turned toward the door. Minerva walked with me, half a step behind. We went through the door together but when I slammed it shut she was gone.

Gone. Not there . . . as if she had never been there. This didn't surprise me. There was something about Minerva that was just beyond what I could reach or touch.

I looked around quickly but there was no sign of her. I unlocked the door and went back into the storage area. When the lights came on I looked at the footprints left on the dusty concrete—only my small shoes had left any impression there.

"*HERE'S THE FILE* you wanted," I said to Stella Furman. She had gray hair and glasses with rhinestones embedded along the frames.

I placed the manila folder in her inbox and turned to leave.

"Mr. Pope," the middle-aged receptionist said.

"Yes?"

"Lana would like you to come in for a moment."

She indicated the door behind her and I took a deep breath before walking through. Just the movement from one room to the other had profound meaning for me. It felt transcendent, as if I had died and my soul was traveling from one level of being to another. I felt ecstatic and nuts.

I had to be going crazy. There was no Minerva. She was a product of my mind. There was electricity in my shoulders, drumbeat music in my mind.

In Metcalf's wide and shallow office I came upon her and Harry Driscoll. She was behind the desk and he was on the other side in one of the two red vinyl and chrome visitor's chairs. I went to the empty seat and sat down without uttering a word. There was something rude about my behavior but I didn't care.

I leaned back against the hard foam of the cushion and looked Lana Metcalf in the eye. She waited for me to say something but I kept my silence.

"Mr. Driscoll informs me that you wouldn't allow him to accompany you to the storage facility."

I glanced at the efficiency expert and he seemed to become a little unsure.

"Mr. Pope," Lana said.

"Yes, Miss Metcalf?"

"What do you have to say?"

"About what?"

"This, this situation."

"What situation?"

"Answer my question."

"I don't know what you mean, ma'am. I didn't let Mr. Driscoll into the storage facility because the rules say that only certain employees of HBH are allowed in there. H. Michael Samson doesn't have access and so he couldn't have given it to your dog here." I had never in my life addressed anyone in that manner. It felt like someone else speaking.

"My what?"

The HR supervisor actually got to her feet. I was sure that I was going to be fired right then and there. But I didn't care. I had experienced a miracle over the last few days. It didn't matter that my experience was caused by a mental or chemical imbalance; it didn't matter that I was mad. Minerva was more important than the reality that Metcalf, Driscoll, and all of HBH could manufacture.

I had to hold myself back from jumping up and capering around the room.

The intercom buzzed and Stella Furman said, "Mr. Hoad to see you, Miss Metcalf."

Before the HR supervisor had time to react the door came open and Mr. T. S. Hoad, Esquire, walked in as if he

owned the place. And indeed he was one of the three part-
ners who still held controlling interest in the company.

Harry Driscoll literally leaped to his feet. Lana was already standing. I would have been in awe myself if I had
not already gone insane.

Hoad was in his seventies and a bit stooped over, but he
was still well over six feet tall. He was gaunt with an aqui-
line nose and green bird eyes peering out of parchmentlike
skin that was color of bone. His suit cost more than my
whole wardrobe. His tie alone was worth a weekend stay
at a fancy hotel. He had thin longish white hair that was
combed straight back.

"Get up, Pope," Lana Metcalf said. "Give Mr. Hoad your
seat."

"Is this how you treat my employees, Miss Metcalf?"
Hoad asked. "You order them around like servants?"

"No, no, no sir."

"And who is this gentleman here?" Hoad asked, holding
his head to the side and squinting with already beady eyes.
"He doesn't look like one of ours."

"Harry Driscoll, sir," Harry Driscoll said, "from Donner and Pride."

"Donner and Pride." Hoad repeated the words as if considering some strange dish set before him at the dinner
table. "I've heard of you. You charge twelve thousand dollars just to walk in the door."

"We get results, sir. We've saved the companies we worked
for millions in operations fees."

"This isn't an operations office," Hoad said.

"Well . . . no, it isn't."

"I called in, Mr. Driscoll, sir," Lana Metcalf said.

Hoad moved toward Driscoll, went around him, and lowered into his chair.

"Oh?" the old man said lacing the fingers of his hands under his chin. "Why?"

"I was, I was worried about the efficiency of the mail-room."

"You spent twelve thousand of my dollars on an issue that is not under your job description or your purview?"

Finally Lana Metcalf was silent.

While staring at the HR VP Hoad said, "Mr. Pope."

"Yes, Mr. Hoad?"

"Please return to your mailroom and try to forgive this unpleasantness. You've done a good job for us for many years and we appreciate that. You've helped train some of our best young executives and even if they aren't grateful, we are. And, be assured, we know that you have always done your job with the utmost efficiency."

"Thank you, Mr. Hoad," I said. For a moment there I might have forgotten Minerva, so impressed was I at being the object of Hoad's attention.

I left the room with the wizened old man still gazing at his VP: a bone-white, utterly patient vulture waiting for a wounded beast to die.

"HEY, TRUE," Pete said when I got back to the office.

"You called your father?" I asked him.

"They fucked with you, man," the boy said. "That was just wrong."

Kala came up and kissed me on the cheek. It was the first time I'd ever been kissed by a floater but the second person to have kissed me that day; if indeed Minerva was a person and not a figment.

I told my friends the story and we laughed together but half the time, in the back of my mind, I was still in the basement with Minerva.

"My dad told me that Human Resources was overstepping its bounds by harassing you," Pete said. "He called Uncle Tad about it."

"Mr. Hoad is your uncle?" Kala said, shocked.

"No really," Pete said. "I just always called him that."

"It's like my aunt Tiny," I said.

"Who?" Kala asked.

"Haven't I ever told you about my aunt Tiny?"

The kids both shook their heads.

"How could we work together for all these weeks and you not know about the woman who raised me?" I said. "I mean that sounds impossible. I think about Tiny every day. I visit her three times a week."

"But she's like my uncle Tad?" Pete the savior said.

"She raised me but we're not blood."

"How come you didn't live with your parents?" Kala asked.

"The first thing I remember," I said, "was being a small child on the street. I was walking, walking. It felt like I had been walking for a very long time. I think I knew where I was going but a bigger kid came up to me on a street corner and pushed me down. I closed my eyes and when I came to I had forgotten where I was supposed to be going."

"Where were your parents?" Kala asked.

"I don't know. I don't remember that far back. Maybe I did know before I fell but then . . ." I was lost for a moment there. Whenever I went back to that, my earliest memory, I felt bereft . . .

"How old were you, True?" Kala asked.

"I don't, I don't remember. All I know is that I must have had blood on my head or something because this woman, Aunt Tiny, said, 'Oh Lord, child, what's happened to you?' and she took me home and washed off my head and tried to find my parents but she never could and so she just kept me."

"Why didn't she call the police or something?" Pete asked.

"Because they would have put me in an orphanage or a foster home and Tiny knew that she was a good person but she couldn't vouch for the city."

"Wow," Kala said. "Wow. That's some story. Did you ever find out what happened to your mom?"

"No. Tiny took me in and I stayed with her until I graduated from high school. Then I got this job."

I could see that my story moved the kids, that I had been lifted out of the ordinary somehow and now had a unique place in their eyes.

I had come to accept the fact that I was an orphan and that no one knew where I'd come from. Tiny was good to me. Miss Boucher was kind. But now, after Minerva, my parents took up a larger space inside. Maybe they were insane too. Maybe they'd been institutionalized and, somehow, I escaped the people who had committed them. I imagined my mother secreting me under the floorboards in some closet while the authorities came to take her and my father away. Maybe they were languishing in some Bedlam while I walked down skyscraper halls delivering mail. My parents were lost to me and I didn't even know where to begin looking for them.

"You should find your parents," Kala said as if she occupied that place in my mind too.

"Yeah," I said. "I sure should. But we got to get this mail out right now. Too many interruptions today. Thanks for your help, Pete, but we got to get to work."

PETE AND KALA, individually, were the best floaters I ever had. Together they were perfect. They did double-time bringing mail to the recipients on the various floors. I did my route and then started going through the paperwork that I had at the end of every day. I wanted to get everything perfect because working at HBH, crazy or not, had been the most important thing in my life for many years. I didn't want to lose that job over some lapse of sanity. Mr. T. S. Hoad, Esquire, had given me a reprieve—I intended to take advantage of that.

A BLISSFULLY UNEVENTFUL afternoon descended upon me. I decided to clean out my desk just after four thirty. There were things in the top drawer that I hadn't seen or thought about for years. There was a huge magnifying glass with a wicker handle that I bought in a thrift shop on lower Fifth Avenue and an old Ethiopian Bible written on goat parchment that was illustrated with red and blue and yellow depictions of the saints. There was a stack of blank Bible paper that I'd bought from a small shop on Bowery and a paper cylinder of wax matches that I got from someone who had gotten them in Italy, from a restaurant near the Vatican they'd said. There were many meaningless keys and candy wrappers, pencils, dried-up ink pens, erasers, and various staples, straight pins, and other office supplies.

There was also a pink envelope addressed to me and sent through interoffice mail. It was from Cindy Brickerman. It must have been nearly twenty years ago I'd gotten that letter. It was delivered two days after Cindy had left HBH.

Dear, dear Truman,

I'm writing you this note to thank you for helping me figure out some things last month. I don't think you can understand how much you did for me that day. You were so kind and it was like you made a little space for me at that cluttered sorting table of yours. Kind of like you sorted me out the same way you did the interoffice mail.

I started thinking when I spoke to you and after a few weeks it came to me that I was going about everything the wrong way. What was it you said? If people would just ask themselves what it was they wanted then they could get up tomorrow and go that way.

I'm doing that now. I'm leaving America and going to Korea to be a teacher of English. That's the first thing.

Thank you so much for your help

Love,

C

I had run across Cindy sitting on a bus stop bench a few blocks away from work. At that time I used to take a walk during my lunch break. That was before I was made manager and they had a floaters program. My boss back then was a man from Martinique named Gerard "Popo" Chosez. Gerard was a nice guy but he was noisy and spent the entire lunchtime laughing or shouting at his wife and then his girlfriend on the phone. I'd take my sandwich and eat it while watching life as it unfolded up and down the crowded Midtown streets.

Cindy was a skinny young white woman who had gone to some fancy college and already had her own office. I had met her on her first day at the job. She was lost and I walked her to the place where the orientation was being held. Even though I'd forgotten her name when she was crying on that bench, I remembered her and couldn't just walk away.

"What's wrong?" I asked, taking the seat next to her.

"I, I, I don't even know." She tried to laugh at how ridiculous that must have sounded but instead more tears flowed out.

I put my arms around her as Tiny had always done for me when I was distraught. I cried a lot as a child because the other children so often made fun of me.

Cindy Brickerman grabbed on to me and sobbed. I had nothing to say. I didn't even remember her name and so I sat there and held her thinking about how generous and loving my adoptive aunt had been.

After a few minutes the crying subsided a bit and Cindy's grip loosened.

"You don't know why you're crying?" I asked.

"John Hightower called me into his office today," she told me. "He said that I was going to be put in charge of my department. Shauna Finn is leaving and, and he wants me to take her place."

She grabbed on tight again and cried some more. I held on as the lunch hour faded away.

"What's wrong with a promotion?" I asked after a bit. "Don't you feel like you can do the job?"

"It's not that. I don't know. I'm just so stupid. I know this is a good job and that I should be happy. My parents are so proud of me. But I don't care about investment possibilities in Zimbabwe or how much oil there is in the ground under Venezuela. I only want, want . . ."

"What is it that you want?" I asked.

I leaned back and looked her in the eye.

"I don't know," she said, "not exactly. I want my life to mean something. You know?"

The words were like an old favorite song in my mind. It wasn't that I shared her desire but that I also felt that life didn't mean much to anyone outside of physical needs and the emotional reactions to those needs. One could walk one way just as well as another, marry one spouse or stay single, raise a family or go off to war. It was all the same in the end—and on the way to the end too.

"Yeah," I said, "yes I do understand. It's very often that I say to myself that people should just ask themselves what they want and get up and go that way."

Cindy was staring into my eyes and I felt something deep down inside me; something like an eruption, maybe even a solar flare. Cindy gasped, I remember. She was lookıng at me as if I had become something else while sitting there.

"That's true, isn't it?" she said. "It's like turning your head or looking up."

We remained in that loose embrace for a few minutes more and then, without saying a word, we got up and walked back toward work. For a block or so we held hands. It wasn't anything amorous. We just felt close.

Once, a week later, she came down to the mailroom to visit. The magic of our connection, though not gone, was muted. That didn't seem to matter though. She brought me a small box of four chocolates and said thank you.

Gerard made insinuations for the rest of the afternoon.

"Truman gettin' a little something from that white girl," he said as if there was a third person in the room.

A few weeks later the little pink envelope came and I kept it in the drawer to remember how sweet life could be even while being meaningless.

The phone rang startling me.

"True?" Olive Breve said.

It took me a moment to reorient myself and to remember who the voice belonged to and why she would be calling me.

"Hi, Olive."

"I just called to remind you that we're supposed to be meeting at six fifteen. I remember how you get distracted at work sometimes."

A sound like an explosion on a floor far below went off in my chest. That was the sex I remembered with Olive. She made me happy because she paid attention to me. The sex we had was all her. She was bigger than me and stronger too. The first time at her apartment she climbed up over me and said, "I need this right now."

"I'll be there, Olive," I said. "I'm leaving in a few minutes."

"*OVER HERE, TRUE.*"

The coffee shop was crowded but Olive had taken a seat by the window. There were two large paper cups sitting on her table. I remember thinking that this was the best Olive. She looked the way she had midway in our brief relationship. She was larger than the last time I saw her but not nearly as heavy as when we first met. It was the moment that she began to see that she could achieve her goal and become the image she had in her mind. That was when she was the happiest and I was still an important part of her life.

I remembered the nights when I was sound asleep and the phone would ring. I'd wake up and see that it was midnight or later and Olive would be there on the line.

"I'm downstairs, True," she'd say, "and I'm comin' to get ya."

I SAT DOWN across from her and she smiled. Her hair was blond now instead of brunette and her eyes were brighter.

"What are you looking at?" she asked.

"Your eyes . . . they're . . . bluer."

"That's my contacts."

"Oh."

"I got you chamomile," she said. "You never drink coffee, right?"

"Thank you."

I sipped my tea while she regarded me.

"It's nice to see you, Truman."

"You too," I said.

She smiled at my answer. "You never did talk much did you?"

"I'm a little shy about talking. My aunt Tiny used to say that there's a lot more to hear than there is to say."

"How is Tiny?" Olive asked.

"She's in a nursing home."

"Oh," Olive said with some sorrow in her face.

"It's okay. She likes the people in her ward and there's a window she can sit by. They have a TV and she can watch her shows. I see her at least three times a week. I'm going there tonight after we have our coffee."

"Hm," Olive said, speculating on words I hadn't spoken.

"What?"

"You made a plan to see me with an escape hatch built in." This was the later Olive, the one that was easy to anger, the Olive who needed a man she could show off her new beauty with; a man that wasn't me.

"You're the one who made the plan, Olive. I always see Tiny on Thursday nights."

She smiled and I looked to my right. Sitting there, four tables away, was Minerva. She had on the same pajamalike clothes and was sitting alone, holding a coffee cup to her chin and smiling—at me.

I turned back and saw that Olive was smiling too.

"I've been made a portfolio manager at my firm," she said.

"Congratulations."

"Tristram made partner at Grumbacher and Lewis."

"That's nice. You guys must have a great condo or something."

Olive leaned forward and took my hand. She looked at me with that old time yearning in her eyes.

"I'm so sorry, True," she said. "I never meant to hurt you like that."

"It was a long time ago, Olive," I said, glancing over at Minerva.

She winked at me.

"But I was wrong."

"You fell in love, only it wasn't with me," I said.

"So you don't care?"

It struck me at that moment that something was wrong. Between the madness that was Minerva, Miss Metcalf's outrageous attempt to have me fired, then T. S. Hoad's incursion, and now Olive calling me out of nowhere, apologizing for an affair turned sour over a decade before . . . something was definitely wrong.

That something showed in my face.

"What, True?" Olive asked.

"I don't know. I mean my life's been upside down lately. Everything is happening at once . . . Let me ask you something."

"What?" Olive said.

"I don't want you to take this the wrong way, I mean, I'm

not saying anything about you I just need to know something."

"What?"

"Why did you call me the day before yesterday?" I said.
"I don't mean why did you call me but why on that day?
Right then?"

"I . . . I had a dream about you the night before." She
stuck out her lower lip and nodded.

"What was the dream about, I mean, what happened in
the dream?"

"Why are you asking?"

"Just tell me. Okay?"

Olive leaned back and looked up at the ceiling. She was
still quite pretty and very fetching in her tight-fitting red
pantsuit. She knew that red was my favorite color.

"You were standing at the entrance of a graveyard," she
said, her face revealing surprise as if she had not considered the content of the dream before. "And, and you had
your hands raised up and there was music playing. There
was a girl, a young woman standing off to the side. She was
laughing."

"What was she wearing?" I asked.

"It was a dream, Truman, not something real."

"Just tell me, Olive."

"A, a pantsuit. Yellow. With these green drawings on it."

I wondered then if I was really there in that coffee shop.
Was I in an institution somewhere in a straightjacket between
padded walls? Was I sitting at a table babbling to myself
while everyone ignored me?

"True, what's wrong?" Olive asked.

"I have to go, Olive. I have to go see my aunt."

"But I need to talk to you."

"About what?"

"I realized something after that dream."

"What?"

"That's why I apologized," she said. "When I woke up Tristram was lying there next to me sound asleep. We've had a good eleven years together. He's cute and rich and my parents love him. My mom's always saying that ever since I've been with T that my life has been getting better. And I agreed with her but the other morning, after that dream, I realized that it wasn't T who helped me. He only saw me after the change, after I lost weight and decided to climb the ranks in investments.

"It was when I met you that everything changed. You planted the seed in me. When I said I wanted to exercise you said that we should walk from downtown to my place every day. When I said that I didn't like my job and that I wanted to work somewhere else you said that I should change myself not my job."

"I did?"

"Don't you remember?"

"I was probably thinking about your kisses," I said, rather lamely.

"That's why I wanted to see you," she said, looking into my eyes again. "I want you to take me back."

I was a scrawny, middle-aged black man who had no blood family, who had worked in a mailroom his entire life. But still Olive was willing to throw her lot in with mine

rather than ride the high life with Tristram Charles. It made
no sense at all.

"Don't you want me, True?"

"I don't know why you want me, O," I said falling back
into our old intimacy.

"What do you mean?"

"Am I like a diet plan or an exercise regimen for you?"
I said. "Am I a flashlight to have around in case the lights
go out?"

These notions hadn't occurred to Olive. She thought that
her offer would thrill me, that her coming back, even if it was
after a twelve-year hiatus, was something that I'd jump for.

"But we were so good together," she said.

"You're a good woman, O," I said. "You took me in and
showed me something I was too afraid to go after. You made
me a man in the way women make men."

"You've changed, True."

"Only in the past two, three days," I said. "If you saw me
Monday I would have been just like when you met me in
that library."

"Take me back, Baby," she said. "Ever since that dream
I've known that my life is just empty. There's nothing wrong
with Tristram or my job—but I know now that there was
once magic in my life. In the dream I was the dead and you
were calling to me."

Minerva was gone.

That was a powerful moment. Minerva had slipped away
again but the madness seemed to increase. I felt heavy and
liquid like the element mercury. My breathing seemed to

have deep meaning while the world around me looked flimsy and impermanent.

"I have to go, O," I said with the equanimity of the ages. "So tell me what you want."

"You."

"That's not gonna happen," I said. "I'm not for sale or barter, not anymore."

Olive's face began to quiver. Deep creases formed in her trembling lips.

"What, what if you just came to see me one night. One night. We don't have to make love or anything like that, I just need to talk it all out."

"You want me to help you crawl out of that grave?"

Her eyes cleared and she sat up looking at me with odd certainty.

Instead of getting angry like I expected she said, "Exactly."

ON MY JOURNEY uptown I caught glimpses of Minerva here and there. She'd be crossing the street or going past me in the opposite direction. Finally she was smiling at me from the far end of a subway car. I knew that she was just a figment of my imagination and resolved, right there on the Number Six train, to ignore her.

"What?" a woman sitting next to me asked.

She was young and dark skinned, even smaller than I.

"Oh," I said. "Sorry, I must have been talking to myself."

I expected that at the least she would grimace, she might even get up and move farther down the car. But instead the young woman smiled.

"My daddy's like that," she said. "Sometimes he's thinkin' so hard that he have a whole conversation before we stop him. My mama used to say that he better never get rich 'cause if he did all she'd have to do is invite the judge ovah to dinner an' my daddy'd be committed before dessert."

I laughed wondering if the young woman was really there next to me on the train or just another delusion.

"I'm Truman Pope," I said, holding out a hand.

"Maud Lolling," she replied, pumping my hand like we'd just made a wager. "I didn't mean to say that you were old like my daddy, Mr. Pope. It's just that you reminded me of him."

"I'm past forty," I said.

"But you got a young face and you don't laugh like older people do. It's only your eyes look like they seen a lot."

"A lot of nothing."

She smiled again.

The train was slowing down.

"This is my stop," I said.

There was a flash of disappointment on her face.

"I work at Higgenbothem, Brightend, and Hoad," I said as the brakes whined. "They call it HBH."

"Why you tellin' me that?"

"Just in case you want to know."

"HI, BABY," my aunt Tiny said.

She was watching a TV show. I've never been able to watch TV for very long. The stories jumped around too much and I found myself getting lost in the commercials. But I sat next to the only family I had while she watched the last few minutes of the apparently heart-wrenching drama.

"WHEN I WAS a boy did I act funny?" I asked her when the show was over and we were sitting next to the big window at the far end of the ward.

"Funny how?"

"Crazy like?"

"Uh-uh. You was always sweet an' nice an' helpful too," she said. "Why you ask that?"

"I saw this girl dressed in yellow but nobody else saw her. Later on I saw her again and she talked to me but didn't leave any footprints on a dusty floor."

Ernestina "Tiny" Pope was a huge woman and unable to walk a city block without stopping for a nap. She was older than her years, worn down by hard labor and deep poverty but her mind remained sharp.

"You always saw things," she murmured.

"What things?"

"I don't know," she said. "I didn't see 'em. But you did. You really did."

"Like when?"

"One time, when you wasn't no more than four you pointed up at a clear blue sky an' said, 'They movin'.'"

"Who was movin'? I aksed you and you said it was some peoples that had lived inside the earth but now they were bothered and had to pass on to someplace new. You said that by the time they got where they was goin' that there wouldn't be no more people like there's people today."

"I said that everybody would be dead?"

"That's what I aksed," Tiny said, "but you said that everything is always turnin', turnin' an' that we had to leave these bodies and dreams behind.

"You were beautiful as a child, True, but then the kids and the teachers at school ruined all that. They made funa' you an' called you retarded. They gave you Fs 'cause you knew too much or you didn't care about what they had to say.

"So now if you startin' to see people and knowin' things again you shouldn't think it's 'cause you crazy, Baby. You ain't crazy. You were a gift to me and to the whole world."

Tiny had begun to breathe heavily and I worried about her overworked heart so I changed to subject to the nurse, Sigrid Marcone, who Tiny loved. We talked for an hour or so about Sigrid's wayward son and all the children he had sired by three different women. After a good laugh I kissed Tiny's broad cheek and left for my apartment.

Minerva walked with me down the dark streets. She was luminescent at night but I didn't talk to her and she had nothing to say to me. We just walked side by side—a man and his mania.

PART TWO

WHEN I GOT home I was exhausted. It had been three very long days and I felt that it was only a matter of time before the authorities came and took me away to the madhouse. I was heartened by what Tiny had told me but the fact that I saw things that other people didn't, even if those things really were there, meant those other people would have to think I was crazy.

I fell into bed with all my clothes and even my shoes still on. I didn't take two breaths before falling, corpselike and headlong, into unconsciousness.

I WAS DRIFTING through the urban night sky at a leisurely speed. Far below the city of New York glowed, not from electric light but with the souls of the many. Bright or fading, representing every species and all the colors of the spectrum, I could see them through rooftops and walls, under the streets in careening subway cars and crawling along the tracks. Now and then a bright soul would wink out—an unexpected death. Beings were being born and hatched, devoured and eradicated, coming together and transforming into something new.

I floated high above it all listening to the music of the light like a solitary mountain climber hearing the wind. I closed my ectoplasmic eyes to appreciate the intricate composition as I floated along silently, unseen and unsuspected. I was a shadow in the dark sky, a snake in the tall grass.

And then I heard a mournful note. It was human and so was I. It rasped and bellowed and I began to descend. Soon I was hurtling out of the sky like a flaming meteor drawn to earth from the heavens.

I found myself in a stuffy bedroom. There was one small, weak lamp sitting on a night table, shining on the bed where a huge black man, my age but Tiny's size, slept restlessly. And there next to him a black woman, my size but Tiny's age, sat listening to his moans.

The man, I knew somehow that his name was Arthur Army, was turning and kicking. His body was failing him because of the weight and the alcohol, the cigarettes and various drugs. I saw in his light a man, Arthur's father, turning away, walking away, beyond reach; a man who would not respond to a child's calls. His fever occluded the faces and the words but the knowledge was still there.

In the woman's emerald light there was only the deep and spreading forest of a sweltering swamp that went on and on. She was alone there, an old woman breathing in the rotting and yet fragrant air—waiting. Agnes Landstone-Army was the last surviving person in her mind. Her parents were dead and her husband was gone, Arthur had become like a wild animal and her friend, Dot, was somewhere down south sitting in a room trying hard to remember her own name.

I was there but with less of a presence than the silverfish

that scuttled, little swirling lines of platinum light, under the worn carpeting on the floor. I experienced Arthur's and Agnes's pains and losses. I felt like crying but knew that this would be an insult to these people's agony. So instead I reached out to them. And though I was unfelt and unseen my body linked the fevered Arthur and the soul-dead Agnes. They came together in the forest.

"Mama?"

"Yes, son?"

"Where are we?"

"All the way back in Eden, child. All the way back before there was even a Adam or a Eve, before the serpent, before God . . ."

"Ain't that blasphemy, Mama, to say that there was sumpin' before God?"

"I cain't he'p what I know in my mind, Arty," Agnes Landstone-Army said.

She was sitting on a chair set among the high roots of a giant cypress while Arthur stood waist deep in lukewarm swamp water.

"Mama?"

"Yes, child."

"I'm sorry for all the things I done and all the things I put you through. I'm sorry for puttin' you here where there ain't even no God to comfort you."

Before this Agnes's face was wizened and hard but now there was a hint of softness. I wondered what she would say. Would she forgive him? Would he wake up and hold her? Would he give her the same kind of support that she had given him through his drug addictions and prison sentences,

his five illegitimate children and all her boyfriends that he drove away?

But another note, this one strident and insistent, called to me. It was all the way downtown. The power of the call drew me away so quickly that I wasn't able to hear Agnes's reply.

A MIDDLE-AGED WOMAN, white with brown eyes and gray-brown hair, was sitting at a dressing table with a pistol in her hand. Through the wall, in another apartment, a man and woman were making love. Down the hall two teenage girls slept in small, closet-sized bedrooms.

Entering the woman's mind I saw that she was looking down into a hole, a deep chasm with gravity much greater than anywhere else on Earth. The pull was inexorable and the woman, Fiona Pinkley, gripped the gun to keep from falling. The only way she knew to anchor herself was to plant a bullet in her head.

This was true. I could see that it was. Fiona's balance was gone, her fall was imminent. I settled down next to her feeling the gravity but unaffected by it. I watched as her mind cast off the ballast of her life: Richard who was at work, Bella and Wendy who slept down the hall, her parents who were in Florida fighting with hurricanes and landlords. It was all too much. Life was a taut and frayed rope that had to break one day. It wasn't death that she feared but the long fall . . .

She raised the pistol to her head and, without considering the consequences, I entered her mind.

Fiona gasped and put the gun down.

"What?" she asked into space.

I did not, I could not speak.

"Please answer me," Fiona whined. "Please."

I imagined a bright red songbird and she did too.

"What does it mean?" she asked.

In my mind the bird became a flock alive with chatter and hungry for seed.

"It's so beautiful," she whispered. "But I can't."

The birds, now acting on their own, flew into the sky above our heads (we were now on an island far from any shore). They swooped around and came back to ground in even greater number.

Fiona walked toward a finger of large stones that jutted out into the sea. She sat there in jeans and a T-shirt with the pistol, Richard's pistol, in both hands. I could tell that she was weighing now with intelligence the right move to make. The red birds, once of my mind but now of hers, settled around her squabbling and playing and looking for food.

I wondered and worried over her decision but before it came I was dragged away again.

THIS TIME I was in Europe, in France, in a small home in Nice where two Algerian families lived . . .

MANY HOURS LATER I rose out of sleep like a drowning man from turbulent waters. I gasped and my heart beat fast. I had been in a nearly a hundred places watching, and sometimes participating, in the tragedies, large and small, of humankind. I had saved some, failed with many, and even participated in the killing of a rapist in Hartford, Connecticut. Always I was a conduit sent, or maybe brought, to short-circuit the lost hearts of man.

"TOUGH NIGHT, HUH?"

She was sitting there next to my bed as Agnes had done for Arthur.

"Minerva," I said. "Why are you here?"

"That's like asking why does the sun rise?" she said. "I'm sure there's an answer but why don't we just enjoy the light?"

"Am I going crazy?" I asked the hallucination.

"How could you be you and not be crazy?" she replied.

"I want to understand what's going on," I said. "I want to know why I'm like this."

"That's why we're here, Truman," Minerva said gently, "to understand."

"Can't you just tell me?"

"Can't."

"Why?"

"Under orders."

"Whose orders?"

"Can't tell you that either," she said with empathy. "I'm here to succor you but you must find the answers by yourself."

"Do you know who my parents were?" I asked, ignoring her fey compassion.

She frowned, squinted, and concentrated as if trying to remember some long-ago event.

"No," she said finally, shaking her head, "I never knew them."

I cried then, realizing that I had been waiting to ask someone that question since before I could remember. Who were my parents? Where did I come from? How could a child one day find himself walking down the street coming from nowhere and headed for Aunt Tiny?

Minerva was holding my hands. Her skin was rough like Tiny's, like any woman who worked hard.

"What do you do, Minerva?" I asked.

"I wake up early and go to war or to my smithy or my library," she said. "I pass the time with made-up duties—waiting."

"Waiting for what?"

"Have I made you sad, Truman Pope?"

"Yes, Minerva. Yes, you have."

"Do you want me to leave?"

There was something in her tone that gave me pause. I *did* want her to leave but that was only because of the trouble I had experienced since she appeared behind me in the elevator. I worried that if I got rid of her now the madness would remain and I would have no outlet, no escape from the insanity. I wanted to tell her, *No, I don't want you to go,* but those words would not come out. I looked up at her—the smiling, yellow-clad girl-child—and shook my head ever so slightly.

She ran a rough fingertip down the right side of my face. The touch tickled and I moved my head just a bit. In that motion I lost sight of Minerva for an instant and by the time I turned back she was gone.

Her departure left me in profound silence. I realized then that most of my life had been filled with chatter and ambient noise. It was rare to have the jangling of the world abate leaving me with the sounds made by my blood moving and the breath moving in and out of my lungs.

There were no words in my memories. I remembered faces and good deeds, Aunt Tiny sitting with me when I had fever and the textural taste of broccoli with melted margarine on it. These sensual memories went on for over an hour as I faced the chair that Minerva had occupied.

It struck me at the end of this long chain of seemingly unrelated thoughts that the chair had always been next to my bed. I used it as a night table but maybe I kept it there for her. Maybe I had those crazy floating dreams every night and Minerva was there to make sure I didn't get lost.

I quickly dismissed this thought as just another symptom of my madness.

DAYDREAMING CAUSED ME to leave home later than I normally did. The sidewalks were crowded with pedestrians rushing to get to work on time. But crowded avenues weren't the only thing different about my long walk to work. For the past twenty and more years I'd walked unconsciously, feeling and observing the world around me with no real awareness, no intention. There wasn't much of me present in those walks just as there wasn't much of me in the night sky of dreams the night before. Few people knew me or even talked to me but that was okay.

Now however I was filled with my own anxieties and frets. Olive and Minerva and Miss Metcalf were there worrying me—each for different reasons. My parents were not there but towered in their absence. There was Arthur and Agnes Army and dozens of others that I touched without them knowing it. I had been to prison cells and boardrooms, AIDS wards and deep in senility the night before.

I had not remembered my dreams before that night. I had never felt such pain.

But in the end nothing mattered. I was still Truman Pope, still walking to work. I was still the mailroom manager for HBH. This was all rock-solid reality and from these facts I gathered what strength I could.

KALA AND PETE were there before me. I was twenty-seven minutes late for the first time . . . ever. But the kids didn't say anything. They had hustled the mail accrued from the night before and loaded up their carts without my help. It dawned on me that I could be replaced in less than a day, that Miss Metcalf could have found a substitute for me and very few of the employees of HBH would have ever even known.

But that reality couldn't drag me down. If the president of the United States died the vice president would take his place. I had the job at that moment and that was enough for me.

———

THE BIG-BODIED HOUSEFLY was still buzzing around the room. It alighted on my knuckle twice as I made notes on the ledger that accounted for every piece of interoffice mail that passed through our corridor-turned-office. I was a resting point, a stepping stone in the long three- or four-day journey of that small bug's life.

I called him Bruno because he was so burly and hairy. I know that he could have been a she but the name fit.

I was thinking about that fly when the phone rang.

"Hello?"

"May I speak to Mr. Poe, please," a voice asked.

"Do you mean Pope?"

"Uh-huh, yeah, that might be it."

"I'm Truman Pope."

"Oh . . . hi, Mr. Poe, Pope. This is Maud Lolling from the subway yesterday."

"Oh," I said. "Yes. How nice of you to call me."

"I'm not botherin' you am I?"

"Not at all. Um, it was nice to meet you on the train." I was trying to remember what she looked like but I only had a body image in my mind. She was slight and young and very dark skinned . . .

"I don't really know why I called," she was saying.

"Could we have lunch tomorrow?" I asked, cutting off any attempt she might make to hang up.

"Really?"

"Absolutely. We could eat at the café at the Metropolitan Museum of Art."

"Is that the one where they got the big Egyptian pyramid that you can walk through?"

"Yes."

"I know where it is. You wanna meet at one o'clock?"

"I'll be there."

AT THREE THAT afternoon Kala, Pete, and I were having our coffee and tea break. Kala's old college roommate was coming to visit her for the weekend and she was telling us stories about how daring Sheila was. She had hitchhiked across the country with another girl in her sophomore year and was arrested for civil disobedience in three different antiwar rallies in and around D.C.

"She has a black belt in karate," Kala was saying.

"What kind?" Pete asked.

"What kind of black belt?"

"No. What school of karate?"

"I don't know. It was a place off campus."

Pete was about to elaborate on his question when the door opened and Miss Metcalf walked in. A definite chill came with her.

Pete glared at her while Kala turned away.

I appreciated the loyalty of my floaters but I didn't want them to get in trouble so I said, "Could you guys leave us alone for a while?"

Without a word the floaters got up and went around Metcalf to the door.

When they were gone and the door was closed I said, "Have a seat, Miss Metcalf."

She resented the authority in my voice, I could see that. But she took a chair across from me and put her hands on the table. She was wearing a one-piece black dress and had a large, roseate pearl hanging from slender golden chain around her neck. She had very little makeup on her pale face and her straight brown hair was not coiffed. This unbusinesslike attire was lovely and so was she, even through the brooding resentment of her eyes.

"Would you like some coffee?" I asked. "Kala brought in one of those expresso machines that use the little packets."

"No thank you."

"I don't drink coffee myself," I said.

"Mr. Hoad's assistant called and told me to come down here," she said, the word "assistant" a burning embarrassment in her memory. "She said that I was to apologize to you."

"It's not necessary," I said.

"I wasn't given a choice."

"Why do you hate me, Miss Metcalf? I haven't done anything to you, have I?"

"I don't hate you."

"You spent twelve thousand dollars for a man to find fault with my work, with my department."

"You left company officers in the elevator while you wandered off," she countered.

"How old was Hester?" I asked. The words came out of my mouth as if I were someone else, someone who was close to Lana.

Her eyes opened wide and she rose from her chair.

"How do you . . ."

"She was," I said, and then halted looking for the relationship in a place that couldn't properly be called memory. "Your great aunt. From Rhode Island."

She began to shiver, shaking hands raised to cover her mouth.

Just then the phone rang. I was in another place beyond that room, outside from even the notion of a room separate from other spaces. I was coming back from a shared awareness where life is an ocean and all individuality merges into and reemerges from the one.

"Hello?" I said into the receiver.

"True?" Olive asked.

Lana Metcalf had turned and was headed for the door.

"Sit down, Miss Metcalf," I said to her back. "This'll just be a moment." Then, "Hi, Olive. I'm having a meeting. Can I call you back?"

"Can you come over to my place Sunday at six?" she asked.

"In the evening?"

"Of course."

"Okay. Where is it?"

She gave me a number on Park Avenue and I scribbled it down, said good-bye, and turned back expecting Lana to be gone. But she was sitting there in front of me again, her eyes filled with tears.

"How did you know about my aunt?"

"Kala and Pete were talking about it," I lied. "I guess they must have overheard something on their route."

Her relief was so great that she didn't question why she sat when I commanded her to.

"Oh. Of course I told the people in my department that I'm going to the funeral."

"You look lovely," I said and she frowned, feeling something in those words. "And don't worry."

"Worry about what?" she said, the old nemesis rising out of sorrow. "What would I have to worry about?"

"When Mr. Hoad calls I'll tell him that you were sincere in your apology."

It was apparent that she had not considered Hoad calling me to check up on her. And now she was wondering if I was sincere in my promise.

But I wasn't worried about Lana and her concerns; what bothered me was my ability to share consciousness with her. If I was crazy, if I was insane, she would not have responded when I mentioned her aunt. But then again, maybe Pete or Kala had said something about the funeral and I blended that into my madness.

"I really am sorry," Miss Metcalf said lamely. "I'm just, I don't know, I guess I was embarrassed by him coming into my office like that."

"I have to get back to work," I said. "But don't worry. I won't cause you any more trouble."

AT HOME THAT night I drifted again. I entered into a brawl between two homeless men—one of whom died. I wandered into the consciousness of a daughter who'd had a withering sexual life with her mother. Her mother had died the night before and she was planning the funeral while contemplating suicide.

I stood by listening to a brother and sister in Algeria plan the assassination of a young man that they'd attended high school with. They, the siblings and their friend, were on different sides of a conflict and, try as I might, I couldn't reach past their hatred.

I encountered many angry, troubled, and lost souls that evening. Pain paved the night with its explosive rages and sad resolves.

My final stop was with two lovers . . .

They were in the throes of passion when I was drawn to their side. They were in a hallway pressed into a corner humping so hard that it sounded as if they were pounding on the wall. They spoke no words and their minds were filled with carnal desire. Their orgasms were simultaneous, loud, and gripping. The culmination of their passion went on for well over a minute.

I thought of Olive and a pulse went through me as if my body were a beating, dying heart.

As they lay there on the thin carpeting of the unlit inner hall I could feel the regret roll off them. She was sorry to have betrayed her husband once again with one more in a long succession of men. And he once more felt remorse that he was not going to be loved for long.

Their sorrow was mild compared to other experiences I'd had that night. I'd seen brutalization and murders, sorrow so deep that even the expectation of death could not ease it. But somehow the emptiness of these *lovers'* lives was the saddest betrayal of human potential. They were hollow cartoon characters hunting mosquitoes with a shotgun. They were waiting vessels with holes at the base. They were aimless and heartless, feckless and a waste. Seeing them I lost heart in my nature and moaned in my sleep.

I turned and my eyes opened momentarily. Minerva was sitting there on the night table–chair watching me closely. My eyes stung and I blinked. In that instant, as was her nature, she disappeared.

I rolled out of bed and stumbled to the bathroom where I urinated and washed off, scrubbed, brushed, and flooded all the nooks and crevices of my human body. I staggered like the drug addicts I'd seen in the night. I made noises and promises but no one was listening to me.

The shaft of bright sunlight through my apartment window seemed weak, ineffective; a failure in its task.

Outside, people on the street impressed me as the blind in the land of the blind, descended from the blind, and giving birth to sightless children. Even the ground under my feet felt insubstantial, unable to support the weight of the sins that humanity perpetrated against itself over and over again like madmen never able to feel certain that they accomplished even one chore correctly.

I ended up on the marble stairs of the art museum, hours before it was due to open. I couldn't get comfortable on the hard surface. I couldn't take deep enough breaths to calm my nerves. I paced and settled, clenched my fists and followed the clouds with my eyes. I watched bugs crawl and fly. I saw a sparrow attack a giant, sickly cockroach as it tried to crawl to safety. My dreams were becoming reality. I wanted to die then and there.

"Hello, Truman."

I had not expected Minerva to come but she had said that her task was to succor me.

"Hey, Minnie, how you doin'?"

She sat next to me. Her scent was like a deep pine forest when the sap was running and the snow was nearly gone.

"You know you take all this far too seriously," she said. "Life is nothing but a series of events unfolding one after another. A man dies, a leaf sprouts from the mud, a lion licks her cub and grumbles—it's all the same as a stone set in the earth waiting for the world to explode."

"But what about the sorrow and the sadness, the rage and hatred?" I asked, certain that anyone noticing would think me a fanatic talking to the air.

"Without distress there can be no relief," she said. "Without bleeding no one could heal."

"But there's so much unhappiness."

"At this very moment a quarter billion children are laughing."

"But so many of them are also dying."

"They are all dying."

"Is there no answer?" I cried.

"There is no question," she replied.

I looked around and saw that dozens of people were sitting on the stairs. Hours had passed. There was an empty space around me—people avoiding me the same way that they covered over the psychoses in their own dark minds.

Minerva was gone again.

———

I WANDERED THE galleries of the museum barely looking at the paintings and sculptures and jewelry. At one point I entered the great hall where an ancient Egyptian structure stood, the building that Maud remembered. Seated there on a marble bench was a big black man who was staring into space with bloodshot eyes.

I sat down next to him and looked at the old stone building thinking that even it was an infant in the ever undulating and unfolding drama of infinity. We sat there for ten minutes or so before I decided to speak.

"You're Arthur Army, aren't you?" I asked.

"I know you?"

"I met your mother once at a social function. She showed me a picture of you. How is she?"

"She cried."

"About what?"

"It don't matter what," he said, somewhat belligerently. "My mama never cried about nuthin' as long as ago as I could remember. She never cried and there she was with her head on my shoulder blubberin' like a baby."

"Why aren't you with her?"

"What business is it to you, mothahfuckah?"

"I liked Agnes," I explained dispassionately. "She's a, a strong woman. I guess if she's crying there must be something very wrong."

"Me." Arthur Army nodded, agreeing with his answer.

"What do you mean?"

"It's me that's wrong," Arthur said. "She cryin' ovah me 'cause I nevah did do right." Army paused for a moment blinking the tears out of his red eyes. "I remembah in the fifth grade Mrs. Gonzales brought us here. She told me that all I evah needed to know was right here in this buildin'. She said that if I could understand what the artists an' the artisans had to say then I'd know everything I'd evah need to."

Arthur turned away from me then to stare at the stone building. I could see that he intended to stay there until he came to some notion of why that structure stood there.

Quietly I stole away, a ghost giving up the haunt.

"MR. POPE?" Maud Lolling said.

I was sitting in the café reading a copy of Machiavelli's *The Prince* that I'd bought in the museum bookstore. The certainty and cruelty of the author had a numbing effect on me. He supported my dark notions of the world but at the same time gave me hope that there might be answers.

I stood up and kissed the young girl on the cheek. This surprised her I think. She moved her head and shoulders back an inch but touched the place where my lips had brushed her skin.

"We gonna eat here?" she asked.

I gestured at the chair and she sat.

We were silent, each gauging the other but not in an adversarial way. We were like children on the school yard on the first day of the year, destined to be friends for life, or maybe just for that afternoon. It was a familiar sensation; one I had not experienced for more than thirty years.

"Maybe I shouldn'ta come here," she speculated.

"It's odd that we meet like this but there's certainly nothing wrong with it. Is there?"

"My boyfriend would be mad," she said. "Well, he really ain't my boyfriend 'cause he got another girl. He don't think I know about it but I do. But I haven't told him and I haven't given him back his medallion so in a way he's still mine—a li'l bit."

"Even if you two were married this is just a lunch."

"But I don't know you so it's like a date."

I was enjoying the triviality of our chatter. She wanted to be there and she was telling me so by saying she shouldn't be.

"If your boyfriend walked in right now you could tell him that I'm your cousin from Salt Lake City. You could say that I live in Venezuela now and that I'm a Baptist missionary among the Catholics and the socialists."

That brought out Maud's teeth. She smiled and ducked her head a little. I really hadn't noticed how lovely she was before the laugh. Tiny and dark skinned she wasn't what the magazines and movie screens would have called pretty but there was something compelling about her. Suddenly I felt that Maud Lolling was a delicate soul and I cautioned myself to be gentle, not too crazy, around her.

"You silly," she said.

"Yeah," I agreed.

The waiter who had served me tea while I waited for Maud came up with flimsy paper menus. He was white and tall, somewhat arrogant with a mustache so thin that if you only gave him a brief glance you might not have noticed it.

"Are you having lunch?" he asked disdainfully.

"Of course," I said. "We'll decide in a minute."

Maud was frowning at her menu.

When she looked up I said, "Lunch is on me."

"But it's expensive."

"I like the atmosphere and the company," I said. At least I mouthed those words. But I was not alone in my head. There were thousands, maybe millions, of voices in there—men and women, boys and girls. I felt that I could be anyone right then.

But instead I became the words that Maud wanted to hear. Why not? She was young and lovely in her way, innocent and on an adventure.

She smiled and the condescending waiter came back to write down our soup and salad, sandwich and chicken potpie.

"WHY'D YOU TELL me how to get in touch with you?" she asked after Trenton (the name on our server's badge) poured our ice water.

"Because I wanted to talk some more but I had to get out."

"Why didn't you ask for my numbah?"

"I thought that if you wanted to talk more that it could be your decision. It's just not right for an old man like me to be asking a young girl for her number."

"I'm nineteen," she argued.

"I'm forty."

"I did wanna talk to you," she said. "Not like some boyfriend, but, you know."

"I know that conversation with you is easy and I usually have a hard time with words. I try to say things and people don't seem to understand or they hear something else and it's like they aren't even talking to me."

"I know what you mean," she said with mild emphasis. "I try to talk to my moms and to Roger, my soon-to-be-ex-boyfriend, and Miss Klein at work but they nevah seem to get it."

Maud told me that she worked at the office of a famous clothes designer, a white woman known all around the world. It was an office filled with women and Catherine, her boss, had taken her in to teach her about the world of fashion.

"She always tryin' t' teach me how to be what she is— like that's what I want but I don't," Maud said. "I wanna be my own kinda person not what that woman want. Don't get me wrong—I think her life is fine for her but that don't mean I got to be like that.

"An' Roger always be tellin' me what to do an' he get jealous even when I know he hittin' it wit' Talia Grimmens. An' then my mama tellin' me that Roger ain't right and that it's good he cheatin'. But it ain't good—it's sad an' it's wrong. Even my girlfriends don't understand what I want . . ."

Lunch came and then dessert. Maud talked and talked. I couldn't have been happier. It was like watching an artisan creating a masterpiece right there at the table. She was teasing out a barely perceptible path that would bring her to a place where Maud Lolling could be herself with the minimum of external contradictions.

"That's why I think I need to go to school," she was saying at one point and then she stopped.

A moment went by and I asked, "Why do you think you need school?"

"I been talkin' 'bout myself for almost two hours," she said. "It's rude to do that. Why don't you tell me about yourself, Mr. Pope?"

Her attention brought me back into myself. I was no longer one of many but just me.

"Truman," I said.

"Why don't you tell me about yourself, Truman Pope?"

"What do you want to know?"

"Where you from originally? Salt Lake City?"

"I don't know . . ."

I told her about my first memories and about Tiny and the trouble I had at school. After a long while of talking she stopped me.

"But this Olive was your only girlfriend?"

"Uh-huh."

"Evah?"

I nodded feeling shy and exposed but still safe in her sight.

"You know I've had more than one boyfriend."

"You're an intelligent and friendly young woman," I said. "However many boyfriends you've had I'm sure there's a lot more waiting on line."

"You wanna take a walk in Central Park, Truman?"

I said yes not knowing that the fate of humanity might have been part and parcel of that simple nod.

———

AFTER SOME TIME we began to hold hands. It didn't feel sexual at the time. We were just old, old friends together once again.

"I had this uncle once," she said to me in the empty northern region of the park. "He was so mean that nobody liked him. My mama wouldn't even invite him to Christmas dinner. But then he got real sick, real sick. The doctor said that he was gonna die. They gave him poison instead'a medicine he was so sick. And then one day his girlfriend called and told us that Uncle Murray was better, that he woke up one day an' started eatin' and the sickness went away."

"And so did your mother ask him to Christmas dinner then?"

"No, but he came anyway. It was just like that Christmas story when the evil businessman turned good. He brought us presents and talked to us and told us that he realized that he had been wrong. Now he's my favorite uncle. He don't understand me too good but he listens and don't try an' tell me how to be."

There was a sparkle and fearlessness about Maud. She was a perfect companion in my insanity. I was sure that she was there and that my life was real in her presence. The only thing wrong was that I was beginning to dread the moment when we had to part.

We made our way to Madison and went to a chocolate store where I bought her hot cocoa.

"Mr. Pope?"

"Truman."

"Right now I'ma call you Mr. Pope before I ask you this question, okay?"

"Okay."

"Do you have a extra bedroom in your apartment?"

"Just one room."

"A extra bed?"

"I have a small couch but I don't think anyone would be comfortable on it."

She gauged my answer, turning it around her mind.

"If you an' me was sleepin' in the same bed," she said, "would you keep your pants on while we was there?"

"Why do you ask?"

"Because I wanna come stay wit' you tonight."

"But you want me to keep my pants on?"

"I don't wanna be your girlfriend or nuthin' like that but I wanna stay wit' you an' keep on talkin'. You know what I mean?"

"Yes."

"Can I trust you?"

"I will wear pants and a T-shirt but I can't say that I'd like that."

"You bettah not."

"SO DO YOU like me, Truman?" Maud asked.

She wearing my pajamas and lying back with her head against my chest. I'd had an erection for most of the night and my heart must have been healthy because it had been working overtime for hours without pain or coronary.

"Can you feel my heart beating?" I asked.

"Uh-huh. But I thought maybe that was like that all the time."

"No."

"That don't mean you like me."

"I have my clothes on, don't I?"

"So?"

"That means I'd do just about anything to keep you close to me."

Maud turned around and put her hands on either side of my head.

"You sweet," she said.

We had talked the entire night about life and how it appeared to us. We talked about the war and starvation and all the lost souls that kept their sorrows buried under falseness and lies.

"When I kiss you," she said, "I don't want you jumpin' all ovah me."

Then she leaned down and kissed my lips and mouth in a way Olive never had. It was deep and soulful and I couldn't help bringing my arms around her. The smacking sound our mouths made caused a tingling sensation in my abdomen.

"Uh," she exclaimed. "That didn't feel like the kiss of a man who only had one girlfriend before."

"You believe me, don't you?" I asked.

"I guess. But you kiss nice."

"I just followed you and anyway you didn't want me to jump you so I had to concentrate on what was there."

Maud smiled and took my hand. She laid the back of her head on my chest again and we lay there in the glow of our odd meeting.

I sighed and she squeezed my fingers.

"I'm sorry about this, Mister, I mean, Truman."

"Sorry you came?"

"Uh-uh. I'm happy to be here with you. I feel real good in this bed with you. But I know a man wants somethin' else. I know you wanna get wit' me."

A tremulous ripple went through my chest, I grunted and held her hand even more tightly. She pressed her head and shoulders down against me in response.

"I've been waiting for something to happen for my entire life," I said. "A window to open, a light to shine in. I walk down the streets looking at bugs and birds and all the different people. Sometimes I feel that I'm up there in the middle of the sky looking down on the world."

"Is that because a' you not havin' any real parents?" she asked.

"I don't know. I just keep on looking. And so waiting for you to say now or never is just another street to walk down."

"Do you mind how long it take?"

"No, I'm happier right now than I have ever been."

"Could you be happier?"

"No."

"Not even if I said yes?"

"Not even then. You see I'm not here waiting *for* you, I'm waiting *with* you."

Maud turned and kissed me again. Then she laid down next to me, turned her back, and fell to sleep.

*T*WO PEOPLE WERE screaming. Maud was shouting something that seemed important but the other person was drowning her out with his frightened yells. I opened my eyes to see Maud was holding me by the arms. I was the man hollering and she was shaking me, trying to drag me out of the dream.

"It's okay, Truman!" she yelled. "It's okay!"

My heart was thundering. My throat hurt from the strain. I was panting and desperate. Then I looked into Maud's dark eyes.

"What happened?" she asked.

"Nightmares."

"What did you see?"

"Let's go down to the coffee shop. I'll tell you down there."

While Maud was changing in the bathroom I slumped down over folded legs and wept.

"WHAT WAS IT?" she asked at the counter of Metro Diner on Second Avenue.

I had tea with cornflakes and she pancakes with hot chocolate.

"I was in a, in a bedroom where a black man and a white woman were lying in bed," I said. "They were naked, asleep. The covers had been thrown off and somehow I knew that they had been having sex all night."

"Maybe that was what you wanted for us," Maud said. "Only I'm not white and we didn't do nuthin'."

I heard her and registered the words but the dream flowed out of me right around her interpretations.

"They were asleep but not alone in the room. I was there

but there were dozens of other men and women all of them black and murdered."

"Dead people?"

"Murdered by the man," I said. "Tortured, raped, strangled, shot, and bludgeoned. Some had been left to starve to death in subterranean rooms while others were blinded before being executed. As many victims as there were packed into that room there were so many more outside wanting get at him. But they were all dead, impotent, unable to touch or even to call out to the living.

"One woman was trying to get at the man. When she brushed my shoulder I saw her last moments. He had tied her to a pole and forced her to watch while his men beat her father down into death. She was yelling and screaming the whole time. She wouldn't stop even though her father was gone. The man tried to talk to her but she wouldn't stop shouting and so he cut her throat. It took her only a few seconds to die but it seemed like longer. For the span of those eternal seconds she was trying to wish herself free and whole so that she might destroy that man."

"Shit," Maud Lolling said.

"Everyone in the room was like that," I said. "They all had terrible stories that came together around the sleeping, peaceful man. I reached out with one arm connecting myself with everyone in that room and everyone waiting to get in. And when I felt all of their pain I laid my other hand on the sleeping man's brow. A second passed and then another. The victims all stared, waiting. And then suddenly the man jumped up filled with the fears and feelings he had made in his years with the Tonton Macoute. He suffered the pain of

the crushed baby skulls and the rape victims, the broken men and severed limbs. He shouted, 'Forgive!' and ran to the balcony right out into the night air fifty-six stories above the street."

Maud had taken my hand.

"And did you feel everything that he felt?" she asked.

I nodded, swallowing hard.

"That's a real nightmare," she said.

"Thanks for pulling me out of it," I said. "I was with him on that fall. I wanted to die just like he did."

"I'm sorry," she said. "If I hadn't been playin' wit' you like that maybe you woulda dreamed about flowers or sumpin'."

"No. I have dreams like that every night lately. They feel so real."

"How come?"

"I don't know. It's like I'm goin' crazy."

"Maybe you should see a doctor."

"If it goes on," I said, reviving from the tea and the child sitting with me, so concerned. And then, to change the subject, I asked, "What do think about staying with me last night?"

In the morning Maud's face was older and more beautiful. Her eyes had sheared through my fears and more quickly than I thought possible the dread of the nightmare ebbed away.

"It was one reason at first but then it was sumpin' else completely."

I smiled at the riddlelike structure of her reply. I liked riddles. I was no good at solving them but their language and their maddening questions usually made me happy.

"I been stayin' with my mother for a few days and then with Roger a few. I was goin' back and forth and they both hate each other and they both make me mad too. I wanted to show Roger that I didn't have to be with my mother not to be with him and I wanted to get away from her too."

"Couldn't you just stay with some girlfriend?" I asked. "I mean going home with a stranger sounds a little risky just to make somebody jealous."

"I ain't afraid a' you, Mr. Pope. You the sweetest man I evah met. You wouldn't hurt no girl."

I couldn't help thinking that this was what people thought about the mild and smiling men and women of my terrible dreams.

"Anyway," Maud said, "that's what I thought when I got to your house but it turned different then."

"Different how?"

"There wasn't no TV or radio or magazines in there but I didn't care. My mama, an' Roger too, always got music playin' an' the TV on. They always talkin' or on the phone and so are the people through the walls an' ceilin' and floors.

"It's always noise all the time up in their places but it's so quiet at your place and I didn't get bored. You listened to me and told me how you felt. I don't think I could live like you do but it was real nice. I nevah had a man hold me all night and not try and hit on that coochie. And I could kiss you if I wanted. All that meant something to me."

"Want" was not a regular part of my vocabulary. I could go days without eating and years without sex. I found entertainment in the lay of architecture or dust motes sifting through sunlight. I could work twenty-four hours straight and still not feel exhausted and there was no sweetness or salt, drug or alcohol that called to me. I rarely wanted anything but at that moment I had a yen, a hankering for Maud Lolling.

Maybe, I thought, I could get her an apartment across the hall from me and we could have dinner at the diner one or two nights a week. We could visit when she wasn't with her mother or some boyfriend. And every now and then she could come over and spend the night. I'd be fully dressed and she would lay her head down on my chest.

I wanted her but would not say it. Her saying no was worse than not asking. Her laughing at me would have been more terrible than the worst insults and tricks played on me in my years at school.

"It meant something to me too," I said. "I really liked having you with me."

"You ain't scared a' Roger?"

"I'm not afraid of anything," I said.

This was true. I could be hurt, or even worried, but not frightened. Threats rolled off my back and death didn't scare me one whit; death happened all around all the time.

Maud stared at me with eyes so deep and dark. I could see that she didn't believe that I wasn't afraid but there was concern there too.

"I'm afraid a' what Roger might do," she said. "You know I don't think we should see each other no more."

"Why not?" I managed to ask the question without showing any of the pain of heartbreak.

"Because I like you but you can't be my boyfriend and if we stayed friends Roger would beat you."

"I'm not afraid of Roger."

"You ain't seen Roger."

I didn't answer because it was her fear, not mine that we were discussing. I nodded and took her hand.

"I'll always be here," I said.

Maud gazed at me again looking for something and not finding it. She nodded, winced a little, and then stood up from the counter.

"You want me to help pay for breakfast?" she asked.

I shook my head slowly, sadly.

She kissed my cheek and then my lips and turned away.

I watched her leaving tears streaming from my eyes.

"You're making a mistake here, Truman," Minerva said.

She was sitting there next to me in her yellow pajama-suit. The green scrawls on the left pant leg and right arm seemed familiar now. I grimaced, put a twenty-dollar bill down on the counter, and walked toward the exit without saying a word.

Half a block away Minerva said, "You can't make me disappear by ignoring me."

"I eat there three times a week," I explained, "and if I start acting crazy they're not gonna be nice to me anymore."

"Who cares what these mortals think? They're like puddles in the sun, dust on the wind."

"They're people," I countered, "living beings."

"So are flies and mosquitoes, rhinoviruses and weeds."

"And so what am I?" I asked the apparition as people gingerly moved around me on the crowded avenue.

"That's a good question, Truman Pope. Are you ready to answer it?"

"I have to go home and change," I said.

"Do not go to the whore's house," Minerva commanded.

"She wants to talk."

"She will derail your will and pervert your mission."

"What mission?"

"I can't say."

"Then how am I supposed to know?"

"I'm telling you not to go there," Minerva said, all the smiles gone from her mien.

"What will happen if I do?"

"I don't know but it will be counterindicative."

"To what?" I asked though I wasn't quite sure what "counterindicative" meant.

"You must listen to me."

"No," I said. "I don't have to listen. I have friends here, a life. I don't have to be a part of this insanity."

"I'm real, Truman," Minerva said. "I'm the closest thing to absolute reality."

The cast of those words coupled with her tone struck me. It was as if she walked out of my mind and attained reality, where before she'd just been a phantom, a dream. It seemed to me that with those words she gave birth to herself. I was astounded by this perception but that didn't alter my resolve.

"I'll do what I want to do, Minnie. You can follow your own way." And with those words I turned my back on her and walked down the street.

OLIVE'S APARTMENT was on Park a few blocks north of Fifty-seventh. The building was tall and yet old-fashioned, built from rose-tinged stone. I wore black pants and a white shirt with a thin brown tie. It took me a long time to decide on that tie. This was what I wore to work a few times a week but I had never worn a tie to see Olive before, not unless I went to see her right after work and forgot to take it off. But I wanted to send her a message—that I was there as a friend but not a lover. She was married and we were over; that's what the tie was there to say.

There was a doorman with black velvet pants and a red jacket with long tails. He stood up to block my way.

"Olive Charles, please," I said.

"Are you dropping something off?" the clean shaven semi-Beefeater asked.

"No, no."

He stared at me with gray eyes that had tiny green flecks in them.

"Name?"

I was distracted by the beauty of the foppishly dressed white man's eyes. They reminded me of something that happened so long before, something I'd forgotten but, somehow, I felt, the experience had not yet forgotten me.

"Your name, sir?"

"Truman Pope."

To the doorman's left, in a small office area, there was a switchboard mounted in the wall. To the right of the board was an old-fashioned telephone receiver hanging from a hook. The man in the red jacket picked up the receiver and punched a button. He waited a moment and said, "A Mr. Poe is calling for you."

He listened and sneered, then hung up the phone.

"Second elevator down the hall," he said. "Six-Gee."

IN THE ELEVATOR I had the beginnings of an erection. This was always the response I'd had when on my way to see Olive. She was the only woman I'd ever had sex with. The things she had done to me were shocking, experiences I had never imagined. And every time we met she had something new to show me—until the last day when we made love so tenderly and then, when it was over, she'd said, "I've met somebody new, True. I can't see you anymore."

But even this memory did not deter my excitation.

I tugged on the brown tie to reinforce my convictions.

SIX-GEE HAD AN ornate lavender door. There were unrecognizable forms carved into the deep wood. The portal swung open while I was searching for the ringer. Olive stood there in the huge entranceway wearing a short red dress that was tight-fitting on top with flouncy skirts.

"Hi," I said.

Her nostrils flared and she took my hands and kissed my lips. For some reason the erection subsided as I allowed her to pull me along.

The living room had twenty-foot ceilings and a window for the wall that faced Park Avenue. The floor was dark green and medium gray marble with golden, oddly shaped throw rugs here and there. The couches were identical coral-colored shell-shaped affairs that faced each other over an ancient red lacquered Chinese chest. Olive settled on one divan that faced the window. She patted the seat next to her but I chose to sit on the other sofa.

"Are you afraid of me, True?" she asked.

"No, just careful."

"You think I might ravish you?"

"What do want from me, Olive?" I asked.

"Why did you come?" she replied.

"Because you asked me to."

We went on like that for a while, her trying to pull me into some intimate confession and me fending her off.

But I wasn't just talking. In my mind I was climbing a swirled ladder, step by step—ascending, attaining as I scaled the rungs new panaceas of consciousness. I was clambering toward a place that would bring me and my desires into a singular moment where the confluence would be both desire and satisfaction.

"You changed my life, True," she was saying.

"We just walked together and talked."

"I was using you," she said. "You were just some poor guy with a low-paying job who needed his brains fucked out. I never meant there to be anything long lasting between us. I just wanted somebody to love me and I felt unattractive."

"You were beautiful," I said.

"I thought you were crazy mad for me because I was your first. I never paid attention to what you said but somehow I heard you anyway and acted on what I heard without even being aware that it was you who had given me the ideas. You helped me to become what I am and I want you back."

I was staring at her and still on my ladder. I was calling out for an event that was nearly impossible by any estimation. Inside of that moment was the entire history of everything known and unknown, possible and beyond reason.

"It's too late for that, Olive," I said. "I have other things to do."

"You have a girlfriend?"

"No."

"Do you love somebody else?"

"Not like that."

"Then why? Don't you want me?"

"Olive," I said, "you don't need me to get up the courage to walk out of here. You don't need a secret lover or someone to take revenge on Tristram with. His infidelities don't mean anything. Your mother or the people at work or the doorman downstairs don't mean anything. Pack a bag and go to the place where you want to be."

"But I can't do it alone," she said, no longer sexy or seductive.

"All of humanity is alone," I said. "It's a gift and a curse but most of all it is inescapable."

We were completely connected right then, she and I. Her gaze was potent and her desires like a blazing star. I was the focus of all that power. She was the human race and I was one in a trillion trillion possible destinies. If someone was to walk between us right then, I was sure, they'd explode into flame.

The front door opened. It was a good forty feet from the couches but Olive and I were hypersensitive and so we turned together.

I had never met Tristram Charles. Olive didn't want us to meet. I thought then that she was ashamed to have had a boyfriend who was poor and black, small and uninteresting.

I had never met Tristram Charles but the hale and tanned poster boy for the American Way could not have been anyone else. He wore tan pants and a lime-colored short-sleeved T-shirt that fit his powerful torso like a thin coat of paint.

He was rushing across the marble floor toward our pink shells. There was a threat in his stride. If I had the ability to fear for my well-being I might have been troubled.

But even if I had known fear there was nothing to worry about. Mr. Charles wasn't going to fling himself into instantaneous violence. He stopped a few feet from where I sat and said, "What the hell is going on here?"

"It's nothing, honey," Olive said with surprising calm. "I ran into Truman the other day downtown. He's an old friend."

"I know who he is. Your friend Ida told me all about your jungle fever."

I was repairing the ladder in a place that wasn't quite real. It was the final proof I needed to explain my insanity. For some reason I felt that I had climbed into the core of a problem that I had been trying to solve for many, many years—long before I had ever been born.

Olive brought the two central fingers of her left hand to the center of her forehead. She frowned and made a little grunt that was like the deep note of a solitary buoy of pain.

"And you," Tristram Charles said to me, "you get your

black nigger ass out of my house before I tear you a new one."

Now Olive's face was expressing both fright and pain.

"Sit down, Mr. Charles," I said. "Sit down next to your wife and be quiet."

It was a shock to all three of us when the enraged husband obeyed my commands. He wanted to speak but could not. He wanted to stand but instead he sat down next Olive as if bound by gravity and gagged by the flesh of his own lips.

Olive had brought both hands to her head by then. Tristram was glaring at me. I was breathing hard as if having just finished a Herculean task. It took me a moment to catch my breath. By the time I could talk again Olive was lying on her side wracked by the pain in her head.

I stood up.

"A little while after I leave you should forget me," I said to them both. "It would be better that way."

I left the building wondering if I had ever really been inside. Maybe I was sitting in a park somewhere imagining the seductress and the hateful king, the jester in the red tails and maybe even Maud Lolling.

I WAS IN my bed that night reading *Red Harvest* by Dashiell Hammett. It was a book I had long owned but never read. It was about the depravity of the human soul; murder and kidnapping, torture and greed. The hero was almost as guilty as the villains. It was a world bent on self-destruction.

As I read I wondered about the night sky outside the

window and that ladder in a place that was nowhere but soon to be everywhere.

Everything came down to blood. *Without bleeding no one could heal,* Minerva had said. And then there was Maud's relative, the man who had come down with a deadly malady but then had been transformed.

I wondered if the knocking on the door at three in the morning was another phase of my madness. I laid the Continental Op down and pulled on my pants. I opened the door and all that was crazy lifted from my mind.

"Hi," Maud Lolling said.

"Hi."

She came in around me, water finding its way past a blockage of stone. She went directly to my little dinette table and pulled a newspaper out of her purse.

"Look," she said pointing to an article on a middle page.

Haitian Strong Man's Apparent Suicide

Last night Auguste Rauron of Haiti apparently jumped out of his fifty-sixth floor balcony on West Forty-ninth Street. A woman friend visiting him said that he ran from the bed and went straight for the window. Police sources said that they were investigating but that suicide, "was a definite possibility."

Rauron has been blamed for the deaths of dozens of political prisoners in Haiti during his tenure as an officer in the notorious Tonton Macoute. Recently Haitians in Europe and the U.S. have demanded that Rauron stand trial for crimes against humanity.

He is survived by three ex-wives and eight children, all
of whom presently reside in Port au Prince, Haiti.

"I was talkin' to one a' my girlfriends about the dream you
had and her father was there listenin'. He showed me the
paper and said that you was pullin' my leg but I told them
that you knew about it before any paper or news program.

"I tried to put it outta my mind. I even went over to
Roger's house. But he was high an' passed out. All I did was
lie there next to him thinkin' about your dream. Finally I
just had to come here an' tell you. You ain't crazy, Truman,
not at all."

And then she kissed me. We staggered over into the bed
and pulled at each other's clothes until we were naked.
Maud was not a shy lover. She wasn't afraid of germs or passion. I rose to her feeling and cried out. Our orgasms were
profound and straining. Our eyes held each other speaking
volumes while executing silent, almost violent exertion.

"*I DIDN'T KNOW* a man could come that many times,"
Maud said a few hours later. The sun had risen outside and
I was at peace.

Who cared if I was crazy?

"Am I your woman now?" Maud asked.

Mine, I thought. Ownership. Tristram thought that he
owned Olive. America thought that they owned oil in the
ground from Venezuela to Iraq. But ownership and the certainty of death were mutually exclusive. It was we who were
owned, we who were born into slavery—we were possessed

by our desires and our relentless mortality, by gravity and the odd nature of being. We, all the people in the world and me, are temporary manifestations, I thought, moments in time that pass quickly and leave traces that are ephemeral and misleading.

"Am I?" Maud asked again.

"I am yours," I said. "And I will remain that way."

"Can I move in?"

"Yes."

"What if Roger comes after me?"

"I'll send him away."

"He's real big," she said, "an' mean too."

"I think I'll quit my job," I said.

"Why? We gonna need money. I mean . . . I'll work too but this apartment must be expensive."

"I got it from my aunt Tiny," I said. "It's rent controlled. And anyway, I saved almost all the money I ever made. We can live a long time on that and time is short."

"What you mean?" Maud asked.

"The nature of humanity is about to change drastically," I told her. "In ten years this planet will be like a new world."

"Why?"

"I don't know why. I don't know what I'm talking about," I said. "It's just that I have a, a premonition."

"What's wrong, Truman?" Maud asked then. "You seem so sad all of a sudden. Am I movin' too fast for you?"

"No," I said. "You're the one good thing in my life. It's just like I told you—I feel like I've gone crazy. Such wild things are happening that I don't know what's real and what's not. I mean how can I have a beautiful young lover like you

coming to my door and pushing me into the bed? How can
I wake up in the middle of the night and know that a man
across town has just jumped to his death? It doesn't make
sense."

Maud Lolling's intense dark eyes bored into me. I could
see that she was thinking but I refused to speculate on her
thoughts. After a good long while she spoke.

"It don't mattah," she said.

"What doesn't?"

"As long as everything happens one thing aftah the other
then you don't have to worry about if you crazy or not."

"What do you mean?"

"Do you wake up sometimes and you in a madhouse?"

"No."

"Have I been here all night long, every time you open
your eyes?"

"Uh-huh."

"Then it don't mattah if you crazy if everything always
makes sense."

The simplicity of the child's logic made me smile and
then laugh. I was almost convinced by this reasoning but
then I remembered Minerva. I explained that I was the only
one to see Minerva and that she didn't even leave footprints
in the dust.

After deep concentration Maud asked, "Did you evah
ask anybody else did they see her?"

"Miss Metcalf said that no one was there."

"But she she wasn't lookin' for no girl in yellow. Maybe
Minerva was there an' Miss Metcalf didn't see her."

"Maybe."

"So you cain't say if this Minerva is or isn't. But I'ma be wit' you now an' if you see this chick then tell me an' I will tell you the truth I swear."

As I heard these words I began to feel the weight of deep fatigue. I was tired, very, very tired. It felt as if I'd been on a long uphill road for years and years. My shoes had worn out. My clothes were rags and my skin was roughened by the wind and sunlight and hard labor of that endless journey.

I slipped into a deathlike slumber.

My dreams were easier now.

They started with Tristram and Olive having a fight. He was going to leave for Florida, the first stop on his journey to South America and then Africa. But first he visited his lover, a young woman named Gloriana. They went out clubbing with friends of hers.

Olive emptied the bank account she was authorized for and bought a first-class ticket to San Francisco where she was to stay with an old college roommate before flying off to Beijing. Her headaches did not abate but she learned to live with the pain.

I followed them from place to place, seeing into their futures and wondering about the nature of sin. Every time I began to get bothered or upset, Maud would put her arms around me and squeeze until the restlessness died away and I was objective again.

I slept for many hours following Olive and Tristram to Kennedy Airport. They weren't on the same airlines but they were both on my mission. On the plane Tristram felt aches in his forearms and calves, he was assailed by wave after wave of restive energy. More than once the stewardess had to ask him to go back to his seat.

Olive had visions every time she closed her eyes; empathetic experiences of children suffering and dying across the globe.

"True," she said and I opened my eyes.

"What?"

"You have made a great mistake. You have broken your vow yet again."

"I'm free to do whatever I want," I said to Minerva. She was standing at the foot of the bed where I lay naked with Maud.

" 'Freedom' is a human word," Minerva said with a sneer. "You are far beyond their isolate fantasies."

Maud moaned and then sat up.

I looked at her and then at Minerva. Maud turned to me and asked, "Is this the one that no one else can see?"

I smiled and Minerva went pale.

"She can see me?"

"I guess so."

"How did she get in here?" Maud asked.

"She can go anywhere it seems," I said.

"They will obliterate us," Minerva said, no longer smiling.

"Who?" Maud and I asked together.

"The On High."

"You're exaggerating," I said.

"Do you remember now?" Minerva asked.

"No. But I don't care. I don't know how but I gave Olive what she wanted. I have someone that loves me right here."

"Like that fly in your office," Minerva said with a sneer. "This, this thing in your bed is even less than some bug."

"You bettah shet yo' mouf, bitch," Maud said and I loved her for it. She was the girl who should have loved me when I was a child at school. She was the protector I'd always wanted—the sister, lover, confidante, and friend.

"Go away, Minerva," I said.

The violet-eyed, light brown–skinned woman-child gaped at me.

"You're sending me away?" she said.

"I need time to be with my lover," I said.

"But you have destroyed all I have done to rectify . . ."

"Go now," I said and she was gone. It wasn't exactly like she'd vanished but more that she was never there.

"I could see why you think you crazy, baby," Maud said. "That's some wild shit right there."

PART THREE

IT WAS A bad flu season that year; the worst the world had ever known. The CDC finally admitted the vaccine that had been developed was useless. They said there seemed to be at least eighteen discrete strains of the virus that clustered and *traveled* together. The virus attacked the body in vastly differing ways.

One *bug* affected one or more of the senses leaving people temporarily blind or deaf or paralyzed. But these weren't the only symptoms; another one was muscular pain and swelling. There were three or four brain reactions most of which led to comalike symptoms. The flu could attack the vascular, nervous, and respiratory systems, the bones and glands, even the quality of blood.

Children and the aged were the most likely to succumb but they weren't the only ones. Schools around the world were empty while hospitals had to expand into tents anywhere they could pitch them. Hundreds of thousands died while tens of millions fell into their beds and the medical experts around the world feared that this might be the superflu that had been predicted for years.

Even though the world was facing oblivion I hardly noticed. Maud and I spent our days and nights, twilights and dawns so much in love that it seemed impossible. For months we spent every day getting closer than the day before. None

of her family, and few of her friends got sick. Roger came
at me one day when I was walking down the street to the
corner store. He threatened me and then, for some reason
I could not fathom at the time, he abruptly turned and
walked away.

Maud loved me, I was sure of that. She went with me to
visit Aunt Tiny at least once a week and sometimes she'd
go there by herself to have *girl talk* with my only kin.

"I would love you no mattah what you did," Maud said
to me one day when we were sitting on a bench in Central
Park. It was late fall and the cases of flu had risen to over
three hundred million worldwide while deaths had exceeded
eleven million. The sensationalist dailies were calling the
disease Holocaust Flu.

"There's not much I can do," I said.

"I saw Minerva," she reminded me. "And you said, even
before the flu, that the world was gonna change."

I had put those crazy days out of my mind. Minerva had
not returned and my dreams subsided. I was in love and
that was all that mattered.

"I haven't done anything, M," I said.

"The newspapers sayin' that one woman finally got better
from it in Poland," she said. "They say that she could lift
six hundred pounds in the rehabilitation gym."

"Truman Pope!"

I heard my name and knew that the angry voice was
addressing me but I could not believe it. I was in Central
Park with the only woman I would ever love and it was a
lovely day—nothing could go wrong.

"Truman Pope!"

I looked up to see dozens of men and women in and out of uniform with weapons leveled at Maud and I. She grabbed my arm and gasped. I was, once again, trying to figure a way out of the madness.

"On the ground!"

I stood up instead. Maud cried out and I felt a sharp pain at the back of my head. The blackness of unconsciousness slithered with snakes and vipers.

I WOKE UP in a bright and antiseptically white room, bound to a chair with chains, and wrapped in a straight-jacket. The room was large, bigger than most apartments. I looked around as well as I could hoping for a glimpse of Maud. She wasn't there, nobody was.

I tried to conjure up Minerva but she would not come.

There wasn't going to be any escape for me and no relief. But that didn't matter as much as it might have at one time.

I had known isolation and then I was loved.

I accepted the swaddling effect of the jacket and chains and used the time to remember the moments with Maud. She was my anchor and I was her lighter-than-air balloon.

"Mr. Pope," someone said.

My eyes were closed in reverie so I didn't see him enter.

He was a tall man in a black suit; white and sandy haired, the eyes were a little small for his head.

"Yes?"

"Why haven't you or your girlfriend nor any of your families and friends come down with HF?"

I had wondered that myself.

"What's your name?" I asked.

"Phillips."

"Well, Mr. Phillips, I'm not a doctor."

"No," he agreed, "but you are an anomaly."

"How's that?"

"Your blood holds the template for the Holocaust Flu."

"Where's Maud?"

"Tell me about Olive and Tristram Charles," was his answer.

"I used to go out with Olive—years ago."

"You were at her house five months ago."

The doorman, I thought. He'd remember me. But why was I so sure that it couldn't have been Olive? I didn't really remember that afternoon very well.

"Why am I here, Mr. Phillips?"

"You, my friend, are ground zero. We have traced back the worst plague in the history of the human race to you. And we need some answers."

"I don't have any answers," I said feeling that familiar out-of-body sensation I had when learning how to talk with Miss Boucher.

At that moment a dark stone tower appeared in my mind. It was cylindrical but tapered toward the top. Thick black smoke emanating from the tower infected the sky for miles around with its taint. At the base of the smokestack (which was larger than any skyscraper that I had ever seen) was a small doorway. People were hurrying out of that portal, running and falling and shouting out in pain. They were naked and filthy, flooding the countryside as they streamed back toward the world where they had died.

"Don't fuck with me, Pope," Mr. Phillips said. "I can hurt you and I will if you don't give me what I want."

"What can I tell you?"

"Did you have intimate relations with Olive or Tristram?"

"Tristram?"

"Answer the question, Mr. Pope."

"No, no. No sex, no kissing, no drinking from the same bottle. Do you think I have this flu?"

"Why were you at their house?"

"Olive wanted to talk to me . . . Is she okay?"

"What did she want to talk about?"

"She wanted me to help her change her life."

"How were you going to do that?"

At that moment Minerva winked into existence right there next to Phillips. I was happy to see her and smiled. Phillips had no idea that she was there. He kept asking questions and from somewhere my mouth answered but my attention was on Minerva and what she had to say.

"You're a fool, Truman," she told me.

"Why do they have me here, Minnie?" I spoke with my mind as my body gave somewhat satisfactory answers to the inquisitor.

"The Holocaust Flu, of course."

"What do I have to do with that?"

"You created it."

"Me? Are you insane?"

"You took your own divine genetic code, scrambled it up, and inserted it into an inert virus in Olive's body. That's where her headache . . ."

She stopped talking because Mr. Phillips had turned my chair over and now he was kicking me. I sustained blows to the stomach, arms, chest, and head. It hurt but what was bothering me was Minerva's claim about a *divine genetic code*.

The seemingly sane white man had lost his mind. He got down on his knees and started hitting me with his fists. He was cursing. I tasted blood. The chair shattered and Phillips hit me again and again. A shadow appeared on a far wall between my attacker's legs. Feet rushed up and Phillips was pulled off me by three men in uniform.

I looked up, half blinded from the blows, and saw that Phillips had gone completely, rabidly mad. He was foaming at the mouth and struggling with supreme effort. He broke away and came down on my face with his knee and all his weight behind it.

I blacked out.

I AWOKE IN another white chamber, this time a hospital room. I was alone again and in terrible pain. Both legs and my left arm were in casts. I couldn't open my mouth and could only see out of my left eye. I moved my head slightly to the left and Minerva was sitting there. She smiled and twisted her body in such a way as to physically express sorrow.

"What do you mean, 'divine'?" I asked.

"You don't remember?"

"No."

"I should have never let you become Truman Pope."

"I am Truman Pope. I've always been me."

"I would have killed you had I the strength," she said.

"You could kill me now," I offered.

"They can but not I," she said. "And I won't let them do it either. Eternity would be a bleak business without the fool."

The door opened. A woman in a business suit and a man wearing a military uniform walked in. Minerva stood and backed into the wall behind her. I could still see her outline and her violet-red eyes.

The man was black, which at first gave me some relief. I hoped the white woman wasn't his superior.

They both sat in chairs near my bed.

"My name is Olga Rhone," the woman said. "This is General Ulysses Germaine. I'm from the UN and the general represents the White House.

"We're sorry about Mr. Phillips. We were unaware that his sisters had died from the Holocaust Flu. The only excuse we can give you is that when you didn't show remorse he lost control."

She didn't seem very apologetic.

"I haben't dohn nuthin'," I said through the wires holding the bones of my jaw together.

"You are the carrier of the virus," she said.

"I neber been thick in my lie."

"Have you ever been to the Middle East or met with any representative of any foreign power or anyone who might condone terror?" Germaine asked.

That was when I lost hope.

I shook my head as best I could.

For the next hour or so they asked questions and I cobbled

together slurred answers under the watchful eyes of Minerva. My jaw hurt so badly that I wanted to scream. And I was worried about Maud and Aunt Tiny. Finally the pair stood up telling me that they would be back, that I was a prisoner of the United States and that I was definitely the cause of millions of deaths worldwide.

As soon as they were gone Minerva came out of the wall.

"You're a fool, Truman Pope. You said that you were just going to watch."

"Help me."

"Will you listen to me if I do?"

"If we can save Tiny and Maud."

"Your pets?" she said in an exasperated tone.

"Leave then."

"No, Truman. Don't make me to go again. I can't leave you again."

"Then help me."

She smiled and sat on the bed next to me. Reaching out with both arms her hands first rested against my ribcage and then sank below the skin, muscle, and bone. I was blinded and ecstatic. Music of the sweetest horns and the wisest drums played all through me. I sang a song that had never been known on Earth. I moved past a distant star and watched the migration of ghosts going against the tide of the cosmos. I expanded out past the gravity of the Milky Way. And there was so much more to experience—so much more . . .

———

WHEN I OPENED my eyes Minerva said, "The body is cured."

"How?"

"The same way that leaves replace themselves or time turns and wonders about his journeys," she said wistfully. "But now we have to move quickly. The casts and wires and restraints are gone."

It was true. I could open my mouth and move my limbs.

"I can manage the glamour around both of us," she said. "Stay close to me."

I went to the closet and looked for my clothes but they were not there.

"What are you doing?" Minerva asked.

"Looking for my pants."

"Get behind me," she barked.

I did as she said.

We passed through the closed door as if it wasn't there. Military guards were standing on either side but they seemed unaware of us.

"How are we doing this?" I asked when we were alone in the stairwell.

"If I could merge with you we could fly to your plaything's side."

"Why don't you?"

"There are traps in your soul, Oh-Ti. If I were to do any more than heal you I would be destroyed."

"What did you call me?"

"Come on."

WE WERE ABLE to go unseen into a clothing store and steal pants a shirt and some shoes. After that we took a subway into Brooklyn where Minerva brought me to the front of an apartment building on a quiet street of brownstones in Carroll Gardens.

"Wait here," Minerva said imperiously. The tone reminded me of . . . something.

She went into the house leaving me on the street to wonder about who I was and what.

People were dying all over the world and somehow I was to blame. Minerva was real, I believed, I had to believe that. It was possible that I was insane but I couldn't rely on that assumption. I had to do something to reverse and stop and repent my crimes.

I closed my eyes and tried to remember before the day I found myself walking down the street toward Tiny. I concentrated so hard that my shoulders trembled. Nothing was coming but I kept up my concentration.

"It's okay," a strange voice said.

I opened my eyes on a Hispanic man. He was my age and height with brilliant emerald eyes, impossibly crystalline.

"I had that flu," he said to me.

"And you recovered?"

"I can see into people's hearts now. I see other things too. I see that you are . . . special."

"Can you tell me where I came from?" I asked the stranger.

The man stared harder until his eyes fairly glowed. Then he shook his head and said, "Your story goes deeper than I can see, my friend."

"What, what else have you seen?"

"My daughter died from the flu," he said. "I saw the red light of life wink and then perish. And then another kind of shining came up out of her clay and she was above my head and laughing but nobody else saw her."

"What did she say?"

"I can only see, my friend," the man told me. "She kissed me with ghost lips and then hurried off to be reborn."

We stared at each other for a long interval. He was seeing something and smiling even though his young daughter had died.

I saw in him a thousand possibilities. The errant disease could have made him into a dozen different kinds of seers. He could have seen the past, the future, the other, the opposite, or simply beyond. This man, I knew, was a soul-seer, a rare breed of a hitherto nonexistent race.

"Truman," Maud said and I took her into my arms.

"They didn't even see me when I walked out the door, Baby," she said. "They didn't even notice the door come open."

While we embraced Minerva came up close to the Latin man with cut emeralds for eyes.

"Oh no," the sprite uttered. "It has already begun."

The man smiled and touched Minerva's cheek.

"You can see me too?" she asked him.

"Yes . . . very clearly, very well. You seem to be more real like your friend here."

"We have to get out of here, Oh-Ti," Minerva said to me.

———

"... *I HAVE TO* get to my aunt Tiny," I was saying in a suite on the top floor of a Midtown hotel.

The window of our rooms looked out over Central Park. Maud and I were sitting on a couch made for two while Minerva sat on the floor in lotus position with her eyes closed and the corners of her mouth turned down.

"She is safe," Minerva said. "But you may not be if we go out. People are recovering with all the powers of Oh-Ti."

"Are you crazy?" Maud asked Minerva.

"Did I take you out of that room full of guards without them seeing us?" Minerva replied.

Maud went silent.

"What is happening?" I asked then. "Why have you been sitting like that for hours?"

"They know what you're doing, Oh-Ti. They have felt the vibrations even through our disguise. One of the mightiest has sent his soul to smite you and to kill all life that you have made."

"You got a child, True?" Maud asked.

Minerva laughed out loud.

"He has more than one, girl," she said.

"No I don't. I don't have any children."

"What about with that girlfriend?" Maud asked me.

"No."

"I'm going into the bedroom," Minerva said. "Come join me at three twenty-three in the morning. Come join me if you have any hope of surviving."

———

MAUD WANTED TO watch the news on TV. She wondered if our faces would be there with a plea by the police for people to turn us in. We surfed the channels but there was no mention of us. The news was filled with miraculous stories about people recovering from the Holocaust Flu. Though millions had died, tens of millions were on the mend with strange changes to their bodies and minds. An old woman in Cleveland lay down with the disease at the age of eighty-seven. When she got up she looked to be no older than sixteen. A paralytic in Mumbai got out of bed with the strength of ten men. Some people did not wake up. Instead they stayed in their sickbeds talking in their sleep, speaking in different, often unknown, languages telling tales of the past and the future.

One such victim was Ella Lancaster in Montpelier, Vermont. Her brother was being interviewed about her symptoms. The brother and news crew were standing outside in front of a blue-and-white medical facility.

"At first we couldn't even tell what language it was she was speakin'," Elbert Lancaster originally of East Montpelier said to the interlocutor. Elbert was an old man wearing farmer's overalls and a red-and-blue checkered shirt. "Then this one intern doctor recognized some words an' told us that she thought Ella was speaking in ancient Greek. They got this professor from up at UVM to come down and tell us what she was tryin' to say."

"And what was she saying?" the off-screen reporter asked.

"Scary things," the deeply tanned old white man said. "She said that a retribution was comin' down on us from on high. That God himself was the target of evil, that we had to build a great tower to bring back to life those that had been sacrificed to save us. She said that there will be a host of seraphim rising out of the graves of the Holocaust Flu and they would lead and build and plan the protection of the ages. Young people, she said, would rise out of ancient bodies, strong bodies would be given to the weak. She said that it was up to me to open up my land to build a tower that will forge the dead back into living bodies. She said that End of All Days was only a probability but that we will suffer more than any before us had ever done."

The words Elbert Lancaster spoke made sense to me though I couldn't have explained why. I was lost in the world, even more than when I was an orphan cared for by Tiny. The tower Elbert spoke of had been in my vision. The people staggering from under the thick black smoke were the ones who had died from my flu. They had died and passed through Limbo back into life. They would have the knowledge to fight the On High.

"Honey," Maud said.

"What?"

"It's time to see Minerva."

I stood up but was uncertain on my feet. Maud put my arm around her shoulders and guided me toward the door. She turned the knob and pushed me through falling in after because she was pulled by my weight. I believe that was why she didn't shrink away from the chaos of Minerva's lair. After that the door slammed shut and there was no possibility for escape.

It was the most alien place that human eyes had ever seen.

To begin with there was no floor or ceiling anymore, just a yawning abyss above and below. The walls were fleshy and bleeding like a very, very infected throat. These walls pulsed and stank and glowed. We were standing there though there was no floor. It was as if gravity pulled us up and down at the same rate and so we hovered there, weightless and gagging on the stench.

A viscous fluid flowed down the far side of the chamber. Within this stream I could make out Minerva's features. It was as if she was dissipating and being replenished by the same downward motion.

"Welcome, Oh-Ti," she said.

Maud screamed loud and long.

When her pitiful cry was over I asked, "What is this, Minerva?"

"It is the essence of the disease you call life."

"I don't understand."

"You will."

At that moment a whining cry burst all around me. A flash overhead hit the fleshy casing that was my muse. The blast was like a monumental clap of thunder following a solar flare. The power was so great that Maud and I were thrown down.

The flesh of the room constricted around us and a fire, hotter than anything before on Earth, burned, burned.

Minerva cried out in agony and my skin began to peel away. She was dead and I was dying and the roll of flaming thunder beat harder and harder against us. It was coming in a quick succession of waves—thousands of brutal, death-dealing swells of pure power and also hatred.

Maud was yelling out my name and I was crying in the crevice of burned flesh that was once Minerva.

A LONG TIME later I awoke in the small room. The flesh walls were gone. The devastation I expected was nowhere to be seen. My memory, however, was complete. Maud was unconscious on my right and Minerva was dead on the left.

I was numb and no longer wholly human. I lifted my lover and staggered from the room.

"*WHAT HAPPENED?*" Maud asked in the deli.

It was four thirty in the morning and all the hope for the world man had once known was both destroyed and re-born.

In a defunct granite quarry on the outskirts of Barre, Vermont, Elbert Lancaster and fifteen hundred impossibly strong flu survivors from around the world were building the vast Tower of Reincarnation. Ella Lancaster, her eyes like pale opals, gave instructions from a trance that would never be broken. Men and women who revived with gills and thicker skins migrated into the oceans and began new underwater cities sworn to protect the life there. New eyes and minds, enhanced sinew and blood, sixth, seventh, and eighth senses blossomed unseen but potent. Some old people were made young again—blood donors came into being with the ability to cure almost any disease with a simple transfusion or by sexual intercourse—sometimes with just a kiss.

I could see all of this as I pondered my lover's question.

The world was lamenting and not yet aware that they were now a single entity being organized to battle the On High and its absolute detestation of the life I had created.

In war-torn Eritrea a girl in the womb of a flu victim was even now being trained in the ways of defense. A boy in Ho Chi Minh City had just been born. He might well become the master of war; hated and loved, needed and ultimately, if humankind, and indeed all life, was lucky—he would be sacrificed for a peace that would reverberate through the dark corridors of existence; places that the human mind could, as yet, not even imagine.

"What happened to your friend Minerva?" Maud asked.

"She died."

"How?"

"Someone was trying to kill us, her and I, but she fooled them and the assassin's thrust only found her."

"What was that room, True?"

"It's what I really am," I said, knowing myself for the first time in a long time.

"Are you an angel? Was she an angel too?"

"We were the same," I said.

"What you tellin' me, True? Spit it out because I'm real scared here."

"Where I'm from, M, the thing that you would call a mind can be whole or of many parts. I was of two natures. One was a being who was interested in cosmic mechanics, how things worked and what, if anything, was their destiny. The other self was a soldier, a being who went out and did what was supposed to be done—that was Minerva. She hid me from view for more years than the dinosaurs lived. She kept me hidden because our race would have had me destroyed.

"Our people can be described as intergalactic social spiders that spread their webbing throughout the universe. Any planet or system or fecund area of space is taken by them. They prefer a place like Old Earth before any kind of life began but they are willing to destroy any life that does not come from them."

"And you one a' them spiders?" Maud asked. I could sense no fear in her.

"Yes," I said. "I came here, hidden by Minerva—her secret brother. I begged her to let me experiment. After millions of years I came up with the basic genetic code that would allow another kind of life. Something different."

"You created life?" she said, her voice tremulous and unbelieving.

I nodded and looked up hoping for forgiveness.

"But that was billions of year ago," she said.

"After the dinosaurs went down I lost myself in the rainforests of the world. I was told by Minerva that the On High would come and that they'd destroy what I had done. But that was okay because I had been stealthy. No one could have detected the onset of life from my hand. All I wanted to do was live among the insects and viruses, birds and snakes. I did so for many millions of years while Minerva, Ah-Ti, waited for a sign from our people.

"But then one day I found me a monkey. I liked the playful creature and took his body for my own. For tens of thousands of years I reincarnated myself into simian form until my spiritual link to the On High was severed.

"When man rose from simian loins I followed him through the variety of paths. I was astonished by human ability, potential. The On High has only one goal, that's why Ah-Ti hid me from them. But humans can be almost anything. This body and this race is primordial and primitive but I believed that there was more promise among this people than the ones who engendered me."

"You created life on Earth?" Maud asked. "You tellin' me that you're God?"

"Only in human terms of the word," I said. "I was also created. The hierarchy of heaven goes on forever."

Maud stood up as if she was going to leave me but then she sat down again.

"Why didn't you tell me all this before?"

"For a hundred thousand years I traveled among the civilizations and barbarities of humanity," I said. "I was trying to come up with a way to save my children. But I was helpless and Minerva refused to engage. Finally, thirty-eight years ago, I decided to become a human child with no memory of the On High and their ways. I reasoned that if I was only human an answer might come to me."

"Why didn't Minerva stop you?"

"We are one in the same but I was the more powerful half because my might came from darkness where strength always hibernates. It was this darkness, this unconsciousness, that patterned and spread the Holocaust Flu. And I was right—Truman Pope, the little man who everyone thought was nothing, came up with the plan to save the world."

Maud was staring at me, trying to decide what to think.

Was I what I said? Was everything she ever thought or imagined wrong? Was she insane?

"What now?" she asked.

"I can make everyone forget us," I said. "Not in one fell swoop but one at a time. I have the power of glamour as Minerva did. We can live together and weather the next storm."

"What's next?" Maud asked. I was happy because she reached across the table and took me by the hand.

"The flu is dormant now. It will sleep for six years. When it rises again half of the world and half of those who were infected the first time will succumb. The next change will prepare us for battle. Our leaders will be children but anyone with sight will mark them."

"How many will die?"

"Eight hundred million and then some."

"But, True, how can you kill all them people?"

I touched my lover's brow and she saw the great tower billowing black smoke and belching out gouts of newly revived seraphim, as Ella Lancaster called them.

"Angels?" she said.

"Each one will contain a piece of my knowledge and over the next century they will slowly come together. Under a Vietnamese general and an Eritrean sister of salvation the world will rise up and defy the dictum of eternity."

I GOT MY job back at HBH. Mr. Hoad himself shook my hand and told me that the place wasn't the same without me; that made me very proud. They even hired Maud to come in as a receptionist. She went to school again and now has a job on the top floor doing something I don't really get. I find it hard to understand business and most jokes.

At night we sleep wrapped in each other's arms and she roams the world with me watching miracles unfold, religions falling into disrepair, and humanity, my eternal gift, glittering like the brightest star in the sky.

Love Machine

ALSO BY WALTER MOSLEY

WALTER MOSLEY

CROSSTOWN TO OBLIVION

Love Machine

TOR®

A TOM DOHERTY ASSOCIATES BOOK • NEW YORK

For Julia Masnik,
who makes the impossible
possible

ACKNOWLEDGMENTS

In memory of Jayne Cortez.

Love Machine

ONE

"SIT DOWN, MS. KIM," Dr. Marchant Lewis said.

Lois frowned slightly and then lowered herself into the chair he indicated.

Lewis was clad in a crisp white doctor's smock that was at least two sizes too small for his great girth. Small plastic buttons strained to hold the garment across his belly. In the spaces between Lois could see the black T-shirt he wore.

When the big man looked down on Lois she shuddered inwardly.

Marchant smiled.

"Don't be nervous," he said. "It doesn't hurt."

With some effort, he walked around the table and took the seat across from her. As he wedged himself in a button popped off and struck Lois on the cheek.

"Oh," she cried, half rising from her chair.

"Sit down, Lois," he commanded in that rumbling low voice.

Lois regained her self-control and sat back.

On the table between them sat a sleek, silvery box about the size of the multimedia player that Lois had bought just that week. In the center of the glittering box was a red rectangular button, that was half the size of a matchbook and lit from underneath. Marchant depressed the button with a thick finger and two square plates shot out from either side, one for Marchant and the other for Lois. Each plate had a shallow, hand-shaped depression covering the most part of its surface area.

Marchant smiled and placed a mitt on his template. He indicated with a glance and a hand gesture that she should do the same with hers.

"Am I supposed to put my hand here?" she asked, stalling.

Marchant nodded. The fat of his face, Lois thought, made him look more like a grotesque baby than a grown man.

"What's supposed to happen?" she asked with hardly a tremor in her voice.

"Exactly what I proposed to InterCyb," Lewis said. "Through a noninvasive electronic medium I will be able to map the complete neuronal system of your hand, gauging the flow of stimuli with absolute accuracy."

Kim stared at the colossus opposite her. She was made nervous, she knew, merely because of his size. Marchant Lewis was nearly seven feet tall and weighed, she'd been told by her boss, Ryan Lippmann, over five hundred pounds.

Big men had always frightened Lois—ever since childhood. But she knew that her fears were unfounded superstitions based on her own size and the bedtime stories her grandmother had told her when Lois visited her in Korea

Town. The stories always had ogres that were as big as houses with obscene genitals and fingernails like claws . . .

But those stories were for children.

Marchant Lewis was no ogre. He was the top neurophysicist in the nation; maybe in the entire world. The thesis for his Ph.D. from MIT was the complete mapping of the memory systems of pigeons, a revolutionary achievement for any biophysicist, comparable to the greatest scientific accomplishments in history. It was a coup for InterCybernetics International when Lois brokered the deal to hire him away from the government. She had to trust him; her future depended on the success of this man.

But still she hesitated.

"What will happen?" she asked. "Exactly."

"Your hand will be drawn in and the Datascriber will begin its work." Something about Lewis's smile seemed threatening or maybe it was just that Lois could tell that he knew something that she did not.

"Will it hurt?"

"I sincerely doubt it."

"I don't really see why I have to do this," Lois said, trying to keep the whine out of her voice.

"Somebody from management has to," Marchant replied. "This technology is about tactile sensation. How can you justify the millions that you've put into my work if one of you doesn't test it?"

Her hands clenched firmly together in her lap Lois Kim said, "That is precisely why I'm here, Dr. Lewis. Your method of farming out work to different unaffiliated labs makes it very difficult for us to judge your work—and its cost analysis."

"You can't judge without putting your hand on the template, Ms. Kim."

There was nothing else for her to say. She'd put off this meeting for a month already and her boss was e-mailing her daily now wondering, forcefully, *What is happening with the Lewis project?* It was Labor Day Friday and she had plans with Grant, her boyfriend, to leave for Death Valley that afternoon.

Cautiously she laid her hand upon the template.

"Let the weight of your hand rest on it, dear," the older man said.

The moment she let her forearm relax straps shot out from both sides of the plate looping and tightening over her hand, securing palm and fingers to the form made for them.

"What's this?" Lois said, the hysteria fully formed in her words.

"Your hand has to be held completely motionless or the Datascriber won't work. Relax, Ms. Kim. There's absolutely nothing to worry about."

While Marchant Lewis spoke Lois felt the insistent tug of the template pan as her hand was drawn into the silver box. She could feel her heart throbbing like that of a small, frightened animal. It was hard for her to catch her breath. A warm, viscous liquid oozed between her fingers.

Lois was ready to scream when she had the vision.

There was a long and very wide plain of green that spread out for what seemed to be many miles in front of

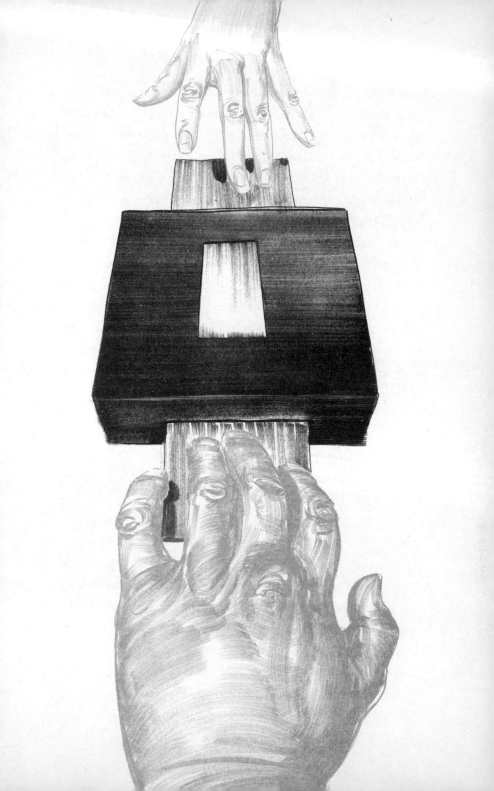

her. This plain went on and on until it slammed into a slate-blue sky. A fluttering of red boomed above her head. She knew somewhere in a faraway place that this was just a redbird suddenly frightened and taken to wing. But in her heart this was an amazing event not unlike when the Lord spoke and life sprang from nothingness.

"Marky," a woman's voice called. "Marky."

Lois cried for joy at the redbird and her mother's call.

Mama never called me Marky, the distant thought chimed. But Lois didn't care. She pressed her hands upon the green, green grass feeling every spiky blade against her tender palms. She heaved herself up making it to a wide-legged stance. A street appeared between the lawn and sky and a big maroon car zoomed past. Lois took in a deep breath hearing the growl of the car's engine and her own breath simultaneously. She blew at the automobile's red brake lights as it got smaller and quieter. She laughed—exultant at her own power.

Cars move due to the internal combustion engine, the faraway mind intoned.

"Marky," Mother called from what seemed like very far away.

Lois spun around so quickly that she lost her balance and fell back onto the grass. The sudden motion of her body, the jumble of sky and green and street made for a joyous confusion that brought her to the edge of fear.

But then two huge black hands folded around her sides and Lois was suddenly like that redbird flapping her arms and legs in flight.

The broad brown-black face—Mama(?)—smiled, showing hungry teeth. Lois felt her bowels clench but she wasn't embarrassed by the sensation.

"Marky," the Woman said again.

"He's a beautiful boy," a deep voice boomed.

The Man standing next to the Woman scared and amazed Lois. This wasn't Dada but still he kissed the Woman. He tried to do the same to Lois but she reared and slapped his big wet lips.

"Benny's a friend, Marky," the Woman said but Lois let fly a stream of curses that came out as one long unintelligible cry. Her bowels opened up and the redbird seemed to be flapping in her chest.

"Somebody needs changing," Mama said and the world folded into flesh and the music of only the Woman's voice and hands . . .

WHEN LOIS KIM opened her eyes she was still sitting across the table from Dr. Lewis. His smile was beatific and she realized, with some surprise, that he no longer frightened her. She had momentarily lost track of where she was and then, with a sudden fright, she remembered the lashes that had trapped her hand. She yanked her arm back only to see that she had already been released. She felt for the oil that had covered her fingers but her skin was completely dry.

An illusion?

As if in answer to her unasked question Marchant held up his hand showing that it was coated with thick, brightly glistening fluid.

"Did you feel the oil on my hand?" he asked in the tone of a much younger man.

"Y-y-y-yes," she stammered. "How did you do that?"

Marchant's smile turned quizzical.

"That's hard to explain," he said. "As you know when nerves are excited they send an electric pulse down a conductor. This pulse transmits data that becomes the semblance of information in the brain."

"I do have a degree in bioneurology, Dr. Lewis," Lois said. The anger she felt also elated her. She was glad to be irate. The emotion somehow anchored her inside her own feelings.

"Yes, of course. That's why I wanted you to come and be the first to experience my little device. That . . . and other reasons too, I guess."

"What other reasons?"

Marchant smiled. He paused for a moment before speaking again.

"My research has found that when any nerve fires a tiny fraction of energy comes free and travels out of the body. This pulse has a very specific, if weak, signature. What my Datascriber does is read this signature, magnify it ten-thousand-fold, and transmit it to the waiting cells of another."

Lois was astonished. She had expected to be presented with a binary chart mapping certain human nerve pulses and associating those excitations with general realms of sensation. It was the overall opinion of the scientific community that actual sharing of sensate experience was at least thirty years away.

"That's incredible, Doctor," she said.

"Did you feel the warm oil on my hand?" he asked.

"Yes," she said. "Yes, definitely."

"Then it has gone from the incredible to the common-place."

For a time they sat there in silence. Lois was trying to absorb the ramifications for InterCyb. This was completely new technology like the steam engine or the lightbulb. The Datascriber would put them in the position to bring in billions of euros on the open market. Her employee stock in the company would double in value within hours of the public announcement. All she had to do was call her immediate superior, Orlando Mimer, and . . .

But if she did that Mimer would take all the credit. He'd go to Lippmann and together they would take the project from her. She'd be cut out of the loop after delivering the report. Lewis would be moved to the company's labs in Mumbai and she would be transferred to some other project; a pat on the head and a ten-thousand-euro bonus would be the most that she could expect.

"Who else knows about the scope of your work, Doctor?" she asked.

"Only you, my dear Lois."

She was taken slightly aback by his intimate tone but any eccentricities on Lewis's part were negligible compared to the immensity of his discovery and her part in its development.

For a moment she was reminded of the vision she'd had, the child called Marky, but she dismissed this as an illusion brought on by unfounded fears.

"Maybe we should keep it to ourselves until . . . ," she said, "until I've had a chance to work out a strategy to approach the board with."

"And why is that, Lois?" Marchant asked, a knowing smile on his dark bulbous face.

"Well," Lois said, "there's the question of the allocation of funds. We're in the middle of an acquisition—Neurotel Techtronix—and of course there's your position on the project."

"My position? Why I'd be the chief scientist in charge of everything, wouldn't I?"

"Yes. But InterCyb always assigns a team manager when they move to an A-level project—"

"A-level?"

"Yes. This is a giant breakthrough. It's so big that there's no telling who they might assign. And the team manager has more say over the project than even the chief scientist."

"No," Marchant Lewis said. "How can someone with lesser knowledge have more control than the inventor himself?"

Days later, thinking back on their discussion Lois realized that Marchant was having fun with her. But at the time she was so amazed by the magnitude of the invention that she missed the subtle change in his voice and the twinkle in his eye.

"It's because their major concern is profit not the advancement of knowledge, per se. They'll put somebody in to make sure that they have some toy on the market rather than a truly advanced system that will facilitate the shared human sensation that your project portends." Lois stopped a moment, pretending to be overwhelmed by the possibilities when really she was just holding herself back so as not to overstate her position. "But if I work with you privately for the next few weeks we can . . . um, position the project so that you maintain control of its direction."

While she spoke Dr. Lewis smiled down on Lois. His responses seemed to be more about what she was thinking than to her words. She felt like a child lying to her mother. The smiles seemed to say that the doctor knew what she was trying to get away with but also that it was okay—he still loved her.

Love? Why would she think about love talking to this hulking middle-aged man, this misanthrope?

"I'm sure you'll do what's best, Ms. Kim," Marchant said in his slow ponderous voice. He folded his hands over his large stomach and smiled.

"So you'll wait until I call before filing your monthly progress report?" she asked.

"If that is your advice."

"It certainly is. There's no reason to blunder ahead if you can get a better situation by taking the time to consider your position."

Lois got to her feet and waited while Marchant shifted his bulk from between the arms of the chair. They stood there for an awkward moment, the black behemoth and the Korean doll.

"I should be going," she said.

"I'll be awaiting your call."

Another moment of silence passed. Lois felt that the doctor's intense gaze was burrowing into her soul.

"Good-bye," she said, taking a step backward.

He nodded gracelessly and she turned away walking quickly through the door of his small rented lab. Just before she was off down the hall she heard him say, "You take care, Gooseberry."

TWO

GOOSEBERRY? GOOSEBERRY? All the way home from
Walnut Creek to her San Francisco apartment Lois tried to
figure out why Marchant had called her that and where
she'd heard the name before. As she parked her jade-green
T-bird in the underground lot of the Los Palmas condo
complex she mouthed the name, seeking, in vain, to remember having heard it or of using it herself.

She packed her travel bag trying to remember as she
looked out of her picture-perfect bedroom window on the
Golden Gate Bridge.

The fog was coming in. It almost always was, though it
rarely arrived.

Gooseberry?

"HE CALLED YOU Blueberry?" Grant Tillman asked.

Even in the driver's seat Lois could see that he was tall
and slender. Grant was handsome with roguish auburn

hair that had just a hint of gray at the temples. He had played semiprofessional tennis during his undergraduate years at Yale and worked as an Antarctic Circle tour guide in the summers. At twenty-three he had started his own software design company making a fortune utilizing Indian programmers to code specialized designs for Russian companies trying to crack Chinese and European markets.

"Gooseberry," Lois said, from the passenger's seat of Grant's Ford Explorer.

They were hurtling down the highway toward Hell's Resort, the world's only six-star spa located in the center of Death Valley.

"I've heard that Marchant Lewis is very, um, eccentric," Grant said.

His voice thrilled Lois with its musical tenor. Even in her distraction she was attracted to the adventurous forty-year-old with the young man's face. This allure wasn't so much sexual as it was a feeling of security, of being sheltered, protected.

"What are you doing with him?" Grant asked.

"Just having a few preliminary talks. What have you heard about him?"

"I had a friend, just a classmate really, named Tom Alex. He worked for Lewis one summer. He said that Marchant was a fanatic, said he'd flagellate himself when he made a mistake."

"Flagellate?"

"Yeah. Whip his own back with actual thornbushes. And if you worked with him you had better not fuck up. Tom said he once saw him throw a woman lab assistant across the room."

"He must have just pushed her," Lois said even though she believed the story, somehow *knew* it was true.

Outside the SUV window night had stolen upon the landscape and the desert sky was hung with tens of thousands of stars.

"That's what I said when he told me," Grant replied. "But Tom said no. Marchant actually picked her up and threw her. She landed right on her butt, had to go to the emergency room.

"But the crazy thing was that when the woman got out of the hospital, instead of suing the asshole, she came back and apologized. Then she begged him not to fire her . . ."

Grant said more but his words faded into the sound of waves breaking on a shore somewhere in Lois's mind. Her nostrils filled with the scent of salt air. A buoy clanged in the distance and then a foghorn sounded . . .

"Did you hear that?" she said.

"What?"

"A horn. A foghorn."

"This is a desert, silly," Grant said with a chuckle. "I was saying that Tom told Marie that she should . . ."

"Who's Marie?"

"I told you already. She was the lab assistant that Lewis threw across the room because her calculations were off by a one-millionth count."

"What was wrong with that?" Lois asked. She was feeling off balance as if she were on a boat looking up at those stars.

"Aren't you listening to me, honey?" Grant asked the beautiful Korean woman.

"Sorry," she said. "Looking at the sky made me a little dizzy. There's so many stars . . . But really, what were you saying?"

"Tom took Marie out to have a drink and tried to get her to press charges against Lewis."

"But she'd already apologized for her mistake," Lois said, again distracted and off balance. "Why would she want to press charges?"

"Because he threw her," Grant said. "You don't think that's all right do you?"

Lois turned to her lover trying to see past the feeling of a sea cruise in the middle of the desert. She had loved Grant in a staid kind of way. *Had loved? Yes.* The infatuation was over.

"Honey, what's wrong?" he asked.

"I don't know," she said. "I mean of course it's crazy to let somebody treat you like that. Tom should have gone to the human resources office himself. I mean an attack, physical or emotional, on any member of the team affects everyone."

"That's my girl," Grant said. "Tom told Lewis off when he quit and all the guy did was grin at him. He didn't get mad or anything. Later on, when Lewis left the university for a government job, Marie went with him. She left the university, didn't even finish her degree."

"Well she didn't come with him to InterCyb," Lois said, feeling as if she had just returned from a long journey somewhere . . . else.

LATER THAT NIGHT they were in bed under the skylight of the penthouse suite of Hell's Resort. Beneath those stars Lois felt that gentle rocking sensation again. When, by accident, Grant's baby finger flicked across her breast the nipple became immediately erect and she gasped. The room was dark and the young Korean felt a grin, a leer spread across her face. She got up on her knees and reached out for his penis. When his boxers got in the way she groaned yanking on the elastic and pulling the shorts down to the middle of his thighs.

"Watch out, Lo," he said. "You don't have to be so rough."

Lois only heard the thread of excitement in his tone. She wasn't listening to his words.

She'd never really liked sex as much as her girlfriends said they did. Men seemed to expect so much from her. She had to please them and at the same time act as if she was jumping out of her own skin with joy. They wanted to feel her orgasms when, though she sometimes did feel something, it was never on the scale of their passions. This was why she liked Grant in bed. For all his height and strength, his wealth and beauty, Grant had an exceptionally small penis. He wouldn't take off his boxers until he was ready to enter her and she could tell that he felt inadequate. In bed he was shy and never crowed or looked at her like she was supposed to be feeling something profound.

But that night, with the imagined boat rocking and buoys cheering and the foghorn calling her name in a deep tone that sent chills down her spine and thighs, Lois grabbed on to Grant's erection like it was very thick and long and she desired him as no one she had ever known. She moaned at his masculine power and grunted when taking it into her mouth.

Grant groaned in pleasure but Lois heard Marchant Lewis's voice. It was Marchant who urged her on, Marchant who told her to come.

She was on top of him, her thighs aching from lifting and falling on his huge thing. She felt the hint of a real orgasm, her first while actually having intercourse, and then Grant/ Marchant called her name but he was inside her mind and not outside on the bed. It started at the center of her being like a fist tightening, drawing together the net that comprised all the fibers of her being. This tightening clenched her fingers and toes. She felt that she was collapsing into that one center when suddenly everything exploded outward. She shouted and barked trying to get her mouth around a name. Her thighs slammed harder and harder against the body lying beneath her. And he was yelling something but she couldn't make it out over the sound of her own voice.

IN THE DREAM she was still rocking. Her grandfather, who spoke very little English, had baited her hook with cheese and she dropped the line into the waters of Lake Tahoe from the side of the rowboat they'd rented. The dawn was a sapphire herald of the sun's hidden blaze. The air was brisk and mist rose from the lake's surface like weightless vipers shimmying in the air.

"What will we catch, Grandfather?" the child asked in broken Korean.

"Baby dragons maybe," the elder Kim speculated.

His skin was a combination of bronze and gold coloring and he smelled like the vitamin bottle on the shelf above the sink at her house. His smile beamed at her and she giggled.

"There's no dragons in the lake," she said in English.

"Shhh, Gooseberry, you'll scare them away."

Lois's eyes shot open, immediately she was wide awake and trembling. Marchant had no way of knowing her grandfather's pet name for her. She hadn't remembered it herself for years.

It was just a coincidence, she told herself. *Things like that happen all the time.*

Lois closed her eyes but try as she might she couldn't get back to sleep. Behind closed eyes she saw the black boy in the grass and felt the ocean rocking beneath her. She remembered making love to Marchant—no, no, to Grant . . .

Lois got out of bed and turned on the light.

For once Grant was naked in his sleep. There were six dark bruises on his tanned chest; places where she had bitten and sucked while humping him. His testicles looked bloated, swollen from her desire, but his member had shrunk down to the size of a tiny mushroom cap.

Hardly thinking, Lois took Grant's keys from the pants that were neatly folded on the bench at the foot of their bed. He always killed time folding his clothes while undressing. This she remembered fondly, as if thinking about a lover from many years before.

She went out to the SUV with her suitcase and, at four in the morning, began the long drive back to the Bay Area.

THREE

*W*HEN SHE WAS nearing San Francisco she called the twenty-four-hour InterCyb hotline, gave her identity code and password, then asked for Marchant Lewis's home address.

She drove home, showered, ate, and then napped for an hour or so. She dressed in a dark blue pantsuit that she wore for important meetings and then drove to the address the hotline had given her.

Grant had called twice but she did not answer.

At 3:00 P.M. she was standing at Lewis's front door.

It was a big, rambling wood house on Bearclaw Court in Oakland. Three stories high it loomed darkly over the unkempt yard. The grass was high and half dead. Three American-made junk heaps were parked in the driveway. There were children's toys and half-empty bottles of beer on the weather-worn porch.

What am I doing here? Lois thought.

For the first time she was resisting the powerful pull that drew her to the mad scientist's doorstep.

She had it in her mind to turn away, to go back to the stolen SUV, call Hell's Resort and somehow explain to Grant her actions. She had almost convinced herself to do so when the front door of the ramshackle house came open.

A young white woman stood there. Lois registered the girl's race because the neighborhood was mostly black and this young woman's pale skin, blue eyes, and blond hair definitely seemed out of place.

"Marie?" Lois said.

"Lois," the petite blonde replied.

"How?" The word came out of Lois's mouth but she didn't know which question to ask.

How did she know with such certainty that this was the same Marie that Grant's friend Tom had said Marchant had thrown across the room? How did Marie know Lois? How did Marie know that Lois was at the front door?

"I was looking out for you," Marie said. "Come in and we'll answer all of your questions . . . in time."

The girl wore a simple yellow dress that clung to her child's figure.

Lois noticed a slight limp in Marie's gait as she followed the girl into the house. She knew that this would be a life-long reminder of the time, when in a rage, Marchant Lewis had thrown her across a room. But even though she felt as if she could remember Marie's pain she also knew that the young student bore no ill will toward, or fear of, the doctor. In Lois's heart Marie understood Marchant so deeply, with such intimacy that it was a feeling much stronger and

more undeniable than love. It was, by far, the most powerful emotion that Lois had ever experienced.

Lois shook her head in an attempt to clear her mind of
these imaginings. She didn't know Marie. All these notions
were just fantasies. She was tired. She had been working
too hard. That was it. She knew that Marchant had be-
dazzled a student named Marie and that she had left the
university to follow him. It was simply an unconscious connection.

And Marchant was sure to have told his student about
Lois. After all, the InterCyb connection had given him a
great deal of money.

Trying to distract herself from worry Lois glanced
around the room they entered. There were couches and tables
set in odd proximity about the large space. Against the wall
to her left, on a polelike stand, stood a big-screen TV. It was
tuned to a news show but the volume was off. The huge
face of a tan-skinned red-lipped woman was relating some
story that was meant to be lent gravity by her serious demeanor.

There was litter on the floor; discarded papers, dust, a
few children's toys, crumbs, and other unrecognizable orts.
There was the scent of sweet fruit rot permeating the air
and even through her shoes Lois could feel the grit that
covered the unswept floor.

In the center of the far wall was the outline of a walled up
fireplace with a mantel above. Upon this mantel sat a very
large and furry white cat. The round green eyes stared at
Lois with almost human curiosity.

They entered a long dark hallway. After a few paces a

lump against the wall leaped up and scurried away down the passage. It was an extremely thin dog. Because of the darkness Lois couldn't make out the breed.

The only light came from up ahead. It was a narrow passageway. For a moment the hysteria of claustrophobia pressed in upon her. The young scientist-turned-technomanager concentrated on the yellow of Marie's dress. *Marie?* She seemed so familiar . . .

The kitchen and dining area they came to was filled with sunlight. Three of the walls were almost all windows; foot-square panes latticed by thin strips of green. The room and the light exhilarated the science broker. It was, once again, as if there was a concrete memory of something she did not know, could not have known.

Three people were sitting on different sides of a perfectly square dark wood kitchen table. One was an orangish brown-skinned man who had a broad face and a big smile. A blazing blue sun was tattooed around his left eye. He pressed his lips together and then grinned for Lois.

"Everybody, this is Lois Kim," Marie said. "Lois this is Javier . . ."

The broad-faced Hispanic man, who was maybe thirty, held up both hands as if in surrender. On his palms were tattooed twin images of Christ, each wearing a bloody crown of thorns and looking up toward the tips of Javier's thumbs.

"Hola."

". . . and this is Frank," Marie continued, gesturing toward a pencil-thin white man who wore a blue-and-white pinstriped seersucker suit, a pink shirt, and yellow tie. His mustache was no more than three hairs in width.

"Hi," Frank said, surprising Lois with the friendliness of his smile.

". . . and this is Cosette," Marie said completing the introductions.

Sitting two feet back from the table the nut-brown Arab girl wore nothing. No older than seventeen, she was hugging her left knee up to her breast exposing a thick swath of curly pubic hair revealing only the faintest outline of her labia and thumb-thick clitoris. After she smiled her greeting she sniffed as if taking an olfactory interest in the newcomer.

The three had been drinking coffee, or maybe tea. They didn't seem to have been talking or reading or in any other way occupying themselves.

The men showed no interest in Cosette's nudity. As a matter of fact none of the three evinced much interest in anything. This indifference brought a low-level panic into the center of her chest. Lois wanted to run but steeled herself. She was already there and needed answers from Marchant Lewis.

"This way," Marie said. She was going out a glass door that, before it was open, was indistinguishable from the wall that held it.

Lois followed the lame blond waif out the door and down a steep stairway that led into a large flower garden of great beauty.

There were roses of all colors and peonies, irises, birds-of-paradise, dahlias, and a dozen other varieties of blossoms both big and small, bright or subdued. Lois marveled at the fact that the flowers weren't segregated into sections but that they mixed together in lovely profusion. It struck her that this garden was the counterpoint to the dilapidated exterior of the property and the disheveled living room and kitchen that served as her introduction to Marchant Lewis's home.

They followed a path of slate stones that curved through the large garden until bringing them to an ivy-covered brick wall. In the center of this wall was an oaken door bound by iron bands. Lois expected Marie to use the wrought-iron goat's head knocker at the center of the door but instead the girl just pushed it open.

Passing into the room Lois was suddenly aware of silence. She realized that there had been the sound of running water in the garden; maybe a fountain or some irrigation system.

The room was a dim, vast library, the size of a single-story, one-family house—if that house was comprised of only one room. The floor was dark oak as were the bookshelves that covered each wall from that dark floor to the radiant blue ceiling above.

Here and there about the room were circular tables of varying sizes. The larger tables had three or four chairs around them while the smaller ones had only one. The furniture was also made from dark oak.

The library was immaculately clean. The floors were swept, mopped, and recently waxed and the shelves were dust free. And the books . . . passing by one shelf Lois noticed that the tomes were arranged by order of their titles.

At the back of the room stood an ivory-colored desk; behind this sat Marchant Lewis in an ornately carved red lacquer throne. As Lois approached him she felt the dread in her chest transform into a thrill. The only light in the room came from a globular paper lamp suspended on Lewis's left. This singular source of illumination gave her the impression of walking out of the night into day.

"Ms. Kim," Marchant and Marie said together.

Marie backed away as Lois approached the big white desk.

"What have you done to me, Dr. Lewis?" Lois asked.

The closing of the door sounded behind, indicating Marie's departure.

"I'm glad you came," Marchant said. His smile seemed to struggle with a great weight. "Please have a seat."

There was a bench to Lois's left. It might have been a piano bench if it hadn't been painted a garish orange. She glanced at the seat and then back to Lewis.

"What have you done to me?" she asked again.

"Sit and I will tell you everything." His ponderous smile warmed a place in Lois's heart. Suddenly she felt at ease as if having returned home after a long and bitter absence.

She sat, perching at the edge of the orange bench.

She wanted to ask the question again but something inhibited her. Marchant smiled seemingly happy just to be looking upon Lois.

"The books," she said lamely.

"What about them?"

"They look to be in order by title."

Marchant nodded.

"Why is that?" Lois asked.

For a moment Marchant got that perplexed look on his

face that Lois felt she had always known. He knew the answer but words were a bother to him.

Finally he said, "Human beings are not only separated by their names. Their sexes and races and languages all conspire to keep them from each other. Their skin and bones and brains and dreams are all so separate, distinct." He said this last word with disgust. "But we . . . we are all one organism, one singular journey through time and space. Our legacy is one of unity regardless of how we feel or pray or die. To list books by the author's name or epoch or even by subject or appropriateness is to limit our oneness, our true selves. If I had my way a library would be one huge book that grew and grew."

Lois was stunned by the vehemence of the neurologist's reply. But even more she felt the echoes of these same sentiments in her mind. She turned her head to look at the books, expecting something transcendent in their being.

"Do you remember that bench?" Marchant asked.

The question went off like a concussion in Lois's mind turning her away from the dark library. *Yes.* This was the bench that her grandfather made for her when she resisted taking piano lessons. *It is a princess's throne,* he had told her.

The excitement of the five-year-old girl shot through her arms and legs and she had to hold back from jumping up and laughing. Regaining control of her feelings she remained on the bench quietly remembering a time when she was a princess.

"What have you done to me?"

"I promised InterCybernetics a device that could, with-

out invasion, provide a full mapping of the nervous structure of the human hand, any human hand," the scientist
rumbled. "Suffice it to say that I have made good on that
promise. Indeed I have isolated the energy signature of every
possible neuron in the human system . . . also in dogs and
cats, pigs, and even coyotes."

"The full range?"

"Full range," Lewis said with a curt nod.

"That's way, way beyond our current capabilities."

"You sure about that, Gooseberry?"

"How do you know that name?"

"I know it because I have been inside your mind as you
have been in mine. At least . . ." He stalled, thinking. "At
least we have had a glimpse of each other."

"What are you saying?" Lois wanted to scream, to leap
up and run from the room. Marchant's intimacy, which at
first put her at ease, now horrified her.

"With the money your company has given me I have created a new era for humankind. All previously held concepts of life on Earth have been irrevocably altered. We
have gone from the monadic oppression in the age of society to the new world of the universal collective."

"What are you talking about?" Lois shouted. "What
does any of that have to do with my dreams? With this
chair?"

"Everything, my dear Gooseberry," Marchant said, his
grin beaming from ear to ear.

"Don't call me that!"

Lois jumped to her feet, her fists up, her muscles singing
with the desire to attack.

"Calm yourself, my dear Ms. Kim. Please . . . sit. I know that it's a lot to digest. And I apologize that I couldn't tell you when you came to my lab yesterday. But I needed an ally and from our research you were one of the few likely candidates that could both survive and appreciate the Co-mind."

"What? What Co-mind?"

Marchant smiled again and for a moment a vision flashed in Lois's mind . . . She was peering into a mirror, at the reflection of Marchant as a young man. Corpulent even then, he radiated the confidence and good health of youth. Lois realized then that the man sitting before her was ill . . . very ill.

"For a brief instant," Marchant said, as if continuing an old conversation, "our minds traveled on a single pathway. Our memories merged. Our hearts knew the same passions."

"How is that possible? No. What do you mean something that I could survive? Was my life in danger when I put my hand in that damned machine?"

With the slightest shrug of his left shoulder Marchant said, "I don't believe so. You have a very high IQ with a stable and quite confident sense of self. These traits put you above a ninety percent possibility for the Co-mind."

"Ninety percent?"

"Yes," he said, "but it is more than that. Because of my . . . the way I'm different, I can read into people. I can see their psychic potentials. I glean this knowledge from their eyes and the way they hold themselves. It's very hard to explain but I knew that you would be a perfect subject."

"Subject?"

Marchant raised his bulk and came around to stand before her, over her.

He held out a hand.

In her mind she had no intention of accepting the gesture. But her hand, seemingly of its own accord, eagerly grasped and caressed his thick brown fingers.

At first touch she was shocked down to a place that she'd not known before—what she would later come to know as the core of her psychic being. There was . . . a space . . . like a field of white light where only she and the doctor existed. Behind the light, underneath its halcyon glow there was a new, exciting, frightening, incredible world.

Then Lois Kim's hand was holding on to a light that connected her to a place where Marchant Lewis, fat and naked, was swimming in the Winooski River south of Burlington, Vermont. He walked out of the water with a full erection. The young white woman standing next to him said, "What's that?"

Marchant, again in the white space, said, "I've always been unable to repress my sexuality, at least before I joined the Co-mind."

Lois wanted to ask what he meant but she found that she didn't know how to speak in this place. Tears came to her eyes with a feeling of compassion for the young Lewis. She felt his yearning and his fear. She also felt him as a memory, her own memory, and then she was overcome by an uncontrollable urge to merge with him. She reached out to touch his bulbous arm.

SHE WAS IN a small hut in a village somewhere in the Korean countryside. A white man in a U.S. soldier's uniform was lying on the wood floor, bleeding. A man and woman hovered above him speaking in Korean. Lois heard them as if they were speaking English.

"We should kill him," the woman was saying, "then cut him up and put him out for the hogs to eat. If they think we're giving him shelter . . ."

"No. No. It will curse us," the old man said.

The soldier was talking too but Lois couldn't understand him even though she knew he was speaking English.

When she looked closely she realized that her mind could not translate his features into a picture. She was looking into his face but it refused to coalesce into an image.

"That's because," Marchant said bringing her back to the white space where they both floated in the heavenly light, "it isn't your memory but your father's. It's a story he told you. You created the whole narrative but the faces are still unknown. You can see that the images of your grandparents' faces are of them in their elder years when you knew them . . ."

Lois was back in the hut. The soldier had died and the faces of the young peasants were indeed old and wrinkled.

"Oh my God!" Lois screamed.

She yanked her hand away from Lewis and fell from the orange bench onto the floor. There she curled up into a ball, rocking herself on the dark wood.

"Lois."

"Don't touch me!"

"You've had enough for now, my dear," Marchant

crooned. "Frank and Javier will come take you to your room. You'd like that, wouldn't you?"

Lois felt exhaustion working through her muscles. She imagined sleep, ached for it.

"Yes please," she said and a world of light somewhere faded into the blissful darkness of the vast reaches of space.

FOUR

SHE WOKE UP once in the middle of the night. The bed was soft and the blankets kept her cozy and warm in the chilly room. She remembered the hallucinations from Marchant Lewis's electric touch. But that didn't seem so important now. She considered getting up and leaving but where would she go? What could she tell Grant, or anyone else for that matter?

Who would protect her if the visions came back? Who would believe her?

"In the morning," she said to herself, "I will sit down with Dr. Lewis and find out how to reverse the symptoms of his machine. Then we'll bring his discovery to the Inter-Cyb board and I will become the team manager."

With a plan in mind Lois felt in control again. She turned over on her left side and settled, breathing in the slightly moldy air of the old wood house.

Her sleep wasn't deep but more like a very satisfying nap. Many of her dreams included the memories of Marchant, however this no longer seemed strange to her. Lewis's mind didn't vie for her emotions. He was more like a book she picked up, reading a few pages before putting it down again.

"Autism," a voice said while Marky was looking up at his mother's stern face, "can come in various levels of severity and type."

"An' you sayin' that my son got it?" Renda Lewis asked, or maybe challenged.

"We believe so," the young white doctor said, his voice affecting a removed professional air.

Marchant saw a multicolored plastic cube sitting on the doctor's desk.

"An' how much do the medicine for it cost?" Renda asked, her face set hard against the answer.

"You don't understand, Renda—"

"Mrs. Lewis."

"Mrs. Lewis, autism is a condition not a disease to be cured with medicines or procedures. There may come a time when he'll need therapy to correct or enhance his behavior."

"Marky is a well-behaved boy, Doctor, you bettah believe that."

"Fixed it, Mama," Marky said.

"Hush."

"But I fixed it," the boy said again. "I fixed it, fixed it, fixed it."

"Marchant," Renda Lewis said in her commanding voice.

The boy went suddenly quiet because he was well aware of the anger in his mother's tone.

He put the plastic toy back on the doctor's desk, catching the white man's attention. Dr. Bernard picked up the perfectly completed Rubik's Cube and turned it around in his hand.

"Doctor?" Renda Lewis said.

Instead of answering the man started twisting the plastic box this way and that corrupting the perfect sides of color. Lois could feel the bottled-up anger in Marchant. He was on the verge of tears when Bernard handed the toy back to him.

Through Lewis's eyes Lois could see the colors: where they sat and where they might be; the path they could take for unity. One twist, two, three . . . thirteen deft turns and all the little squares were in order again.

"See? I fixed it, Mama."

He can see into the mind the way he saw where those colors belonged, Lois thought. *He intuits how it works by looking. That's why he understands so much.*

The dream passed into other strange tableaus that she did not understand. There was the sound of panting and a full moon up above. Someone, a large brown woman, was prattling away in French; Lois understood about every fourth word.

At some point she became aware that pitch darkness had entered her mind. She was in a place where no light had ever shown.

Threshold, she thought.

"Hey you, new girl," someone hissed.

Against the screen of black stood the young Hispanic man from the day before. Javier. He was wearing drab green trousers and a white T-shirt, black-and-white sneakers and the tattoos of twin Jesuses now in the center of his fore-head.

"What are you doing in here?" Lois asked.

"In where?"

Lois turned to look at her bed but all that was there was an endless, depthless night.

"We're in your mind, at least a little bit we are," the young man said. "It's me here because I was the first one in the kitchen to see you. The doc says that you always choose one as the host and the rest are just storages. Usually it's the very first one you see so it coulda been him or maybe Marie. But I guess you liked my tats or somethin'."

"Where are we?" Lois asked.

"I already told you. We're in your head, your brain."

"Am I hooked up to that machine again?" Lois asked, icy fingers grasping at her heart.

"No, man," Javier said. "I'm in your head. When you and the doctor linked up everyone he has in him was trans-ferred to you. Not *all* of us but enough so that we could talk if you want. Me, Marie, Frankie, and Lana. It's kinda like we just met or somethin', like somebody you know only not so well."

"All of you?" Lois asked imagining the Mexican's body crammed into her skull. A claustrophobic panic rose in her body and mind.

"Come on," Javier replied, "I'll show you."

He grabbed her hand and a pinwheel of light trans-formed the darkness . . .

. . . into a small traveling carnival in a desert town somewhere south of Palm Springs. Javier was holding Lois's hand and they were running through a large crowd of mostly Mexican families. She and Javier were small children moving fast and giggling.

"Come on!" the boy shouted, not in English.

Lois began laughing but there was nothing funny going on.

The next thing she knew they were sitting side by side in the front car of a wooden roller coaster, climbing slowly to the top of a large dip. Javier's heart was beating fast. It was as if his heart and hers were one. When they reached the crest the car stopped for a moment and then with impossible velocity they fell down the nearly vertical tracks. They screamed together. The scene blurred out now and again and when it came into focus they were, once more, at the top of the crest just about to fall.

Lois saw that her hands were brown like Javier's.

Images faded into bright colored blurs and then came together again and again in different scenes of the carnival The darkness from the first dream had backed off into the distance but it was still there; it was always there.

They found themselves at the top of the Ferris wheel where they stopped somewhere near the top. Javier turned to Lois and said, "Kiss me, Katarina. Kiss me hard."

"I'm not Katarina," Lois said gently.

The darkness had covered the sky above them but now it was domed in stars. It was so beautiful and Lois felt profound gratitude for being taken to such a place that she'd never been but still it thrummed inside her.

"But you look like her," Javier said.

"Only because you want me to." Lois knew that this was not strictly true. She was aware in some barely conscious place in her mind that she could turn back into her physical form at any time.

"Katarina said no to me at the top of the night," Javier said. "She told me that she loved Miguel and that she wouldn't kiss me."

Lois could see that it was all true. She felt Javier's jilted pain and relented, leaning into his boyish kiss. It felt sweet but what really moved her was the relief in the boy's soul. She smiled realizing that he was holding back from touching her budding breasts because he had only asked for a kiss.

After a long moment she pulled away from the smiling teenager.

"You were a boy when we got on this ride," she said.

"A boy grows up."

"I could stay here forever," Lois said, smiling and taking young Javier by both hands.

"We can stay as long as you want," Javier replied.

The carnival faded away completely, except for the high car on the Ferris wheel and what looked like every star in the Milky Way hovering above them.

"How are we here?" Lois/Katarina asked.

"When you connected with the doctor through the machine," Javier, now the tattooed man, said, "a small part of my character and personality and memories, the important ones, copied into a space in your brain."

"Copied?"

"Yeah. You know most of the brain is functional, not

unique. The ability to speak a language takes up much more space than the language itself. The person you are— the nuances and attitudes are almost nothing. Marchant says that a normally functioning brain can contain fifty thousand personalities and all of their most important memories."

"So if you're copied," Lois (not Katarina) asked, "then can you be erased?"

"Are you tired of me already?"

The sadness in Javier was vast. It was like being brought to the edge of a chasm of infinite blackness. She realized then that erasing Javier would be tantamount to murder.

"What's your level of education, Javier?"

"I dropped out of high school but I hadn't even passed one class since the eighth grade."

"But you can speak so eloquently and technically."

"When I merged with Dr. Lewis and Marie I learned much of what they know. At night, in my sleep, they explain to me how things work. And I show them stuff too."

"Like the carnival?"

"And gang fights and cops and teachers that don't give a shit 'bout no beaner."

Lois felt the young man's humiliation and anger but she was so close to it that it seemed familiar enough not to be overwhelming.

"Did you teach them how to speak Spanish?" she asked.

"There is the one language and there are the many," he said in an odd tone. "Spanish or English or French could fit in a thimble but the One Tongue could occupy every star above your head."

"I don't understand," Lois said.

"You need sleep, Gooseberry," Javier replied. "Come see me tomorrow night if you want to. Maybe then we can talk about languages and all the pieces of people, and others, you contain."

And even though Lois wanted to talk more under the desert skies she felt the psychic tableau fading. Slowly the night turned into another kind of darkness and the dreams settled into dust upon a vast, unseen desert floor.

FIVE

WHEN LOIS AWOKE she felt better, more optimistic than she could ever remember. The sun through her window seemed full of promise. She was naked in the small single bed and her clothes were folded on a wooden chair that sat beneath the glowing windowpane. The sunlight over the chair and her polka dot dress made her laugh out loud. She wondered if Javier and Frank had undressed her but nakedness didn't seem so important anymore. She could list a hundred important things, habits, attitudes, tastes about Javier and if she tried she knew that she could do the same with Frank and Marie, Marchant and Cosette.

Lois pulled on her dress without worrying about the underwear. She went into the creaking hall, stopped to urinate in the toilet two doors down, and then descended two flights into the living room noticing, almost without registering, that the floors were picked up and cleaned.

In the kitchen dining room she found the whole family sitting around the breakfast table. Marchant was laughing, smoking a cigarette. Cosette was still naked and Frank was flipping pancakes on a griddle that was large enough to cover two burners of the stove.

"Marie saw how you looked at the rooms," Cosette said, "and we realized that we haven't been very neat lately. Sometimes we sit around for days following mental paths instead of physical ones."

"That is our greatest obstacle," Frank said, not looking at her.

The Arab-French girl was gazing into Lois's eyes with gray orbs. She was beautiful Lois thought—*but wild,* a voice in her mind whispered.

"Good morning," Marchant hailed looking up from the curling blue and white smoke of his cigarette. "Come sit with me and together we will plan the overthrow of the world."

Lois shuddered but still moved to sit next to the five-hundred-pound scientist.

"*Que pasa, chica?*" Javier said with a familiar twinkle in his eye.

Lois understood that this wasn't exactly *her* Javier but she felt a tenderness toward him anyway.

"Are you autistic?" Lois asked Marchant. She'd made up her mind on the way downstairs to be blunt with the mad scientist. *Otherwise he'll get all slippery.*

"I was," he said carefully and with emphasis. "And in some ways I still am. Did we visit in your dreams?"

"I did have a dream. You were in a doctor's office. Your mother wanted you to be treated, to be cured. But the doctor said that you suffered from autism."

"Bernard," Marchant said. "Dr. Bernard. He took me on as a patient after I did all his puzzles. I had a handicap and a genius and he wanted to map out the relationship between the two."

"And so he helped you become a neurologist?"

"Yes. I followed him to Stanford and became his assistant. Later on I surpassed him and began to do research on my own."

"Mapping the brain."

"Creating the Love Machine."

"Love Machine?"

"What else would you call it?" Lewis asked. "After just a minute of our connection I am closer to you than I ever was with my own mother."

Cosette came over and sat on Lois's lap, her gray eyes staring into the Korean's.

Odors assailed the science broker, bodies and streets, flash rainstorms and lightning. Cosette smiled and her eyes went wide with anticipation.

"Come to my room after you're finished with the fat man," the Arab teenager said. "I will show you how to play."

With that she hopped up and ran from the room. No one called after her or even seemed to register the behavior as odd.

"The world," Lewis said.

Frank, wearing a pink-and-white seersucker suit today, placed a plate of pancakes down for each of them.

He didn't say anything, didn't introduce the food or encourage them to eat while it was hot. Looking at the thin white man Lois realized that he had never cooked before coming to World's End . . . *World's End*, she mused. *The end of the world, the name of this house. The falling of the individual into a mass of histories, destroying what went before. This was the point from which the biblical flood issued where Ghengis Kahn gathered his armies; this was the dream of madmen and popes, and mad popes . . .* Lois came back to the notion that Marie was the cook in the house but anyone there could fulfill her role because they held her in their hearts or, more accurately, their minds.

Marchant was enjoying his third mouthful when Lois came back to the room she was in. Her mind, she realized, had floated off into the possibilities . . . no, no, the realities shared between the people there and another who, though not known, crowded at the outer edge of her consciousness.

"Have you read the works of Lewis Mumford?" Marchant asked Lois.

"The social historian and theorist," she said feeling vast and alone but not lonely or adrift.

"He followed the impact of technology on mankind, humankind if you will. He could explain to you how the advent of an innocuous invention like a certain kind of screw might be the tipping point for vast revolutionary changes in a hitherto stable society. Royal families torn down, political and social relationships completely altered after centuries of so-called social stability."

"I've read his work on the city through history," she said and then it came to her that Frank was a gambler; that he spent long days at the racetrack and night after night at card tables and before roulette wheels.

"Albert Einstein," Marchant said, "delivers a letter of warning to Franklin Delano Roosevelt revealing the possibility of a nuclear chain reaction and then, years later, he laments his role in the creation of the nuclear age."

"Science and society have a crazy unpredictable relationship," Lois said. "I often think that what I may be doing has more to do with profit than a better life for people."

"And poverty and crime and ignorance and prisons and indiscriminate unfulfilled desires," Marchant added. "We, scientists, are like capricious gods creating one Pandora's box after another and placing them before fools without giving them even the chance of a warning. Scientists are the greatest criminals in the modern world."

Marie and Javier were sitting right across from them, holding hands and reading a huge tome, eating pancakes with odd expressions on their faces—each genuinely influenced by the other.

"What's your point?" Lois asked.

"From mustard gas," Lewis said, "to the hydrogen bomb."

"You might as well blame an electron for its nucleus," Lois replied, the sarcasm in her voice was both alien and familiar to her.

Marchant laughed loudly but that didn't disturb Marie and Javier. Together they turned a page in the big book.

"But, my dear," Marchant said, still chortling, "electrons can break free or bond with another element to transform the one thing into another."

"Electrons don't have free will," the young woman said. She was beginning to enjoy the banter. It made her feel that she was anchored somehow, not floating in the ether of mind.

"Neither do humans," Marchant replied. "We do things and those things impact the world. We meet and fuck and make babies who are maybe destined to starve or wage war. That wasn't the plan but we have to do something, don't we?"

"I don't understand, Doctor."

"We are responsible for history wouldn't you say, Gooseberry?"

"Not necessarily," Lois replied. "I walk ahead of you on a mountain path and the ground beneath my feet is weak but I don't know it. My footstep loosens the ground even more and then, when you come along it gives way. You fall to your death but I am not responsible even if I am the cause."

Marchant was smiling, staring at the younger woman. She saw that his brown eyes had *whites* that were a lighter shade of the same color. This simple juxtaposition of color told her that he was dying.

"But as a scientist you build a stairway to the moon," he said. "You don't realize that it has military implications but then a leader, let us call him Chainman, passes a law that America owns that ladder and he places tactical weapons on it and trains them on his enemies. Where does your responsibility lay then, my dear?"

"I haven't built any ladder."

With surprising speed Marchant Lewis grabbed Lois by

the biceps of both arms and stood up lifting her into the air with him.

"I am alive in you!" he shouted. "My mind contains the potentials of an entire race. I have changed the world only it doesn't know it yet."

Lois felt no fear or outrage. Javier and Marie didn't even look up from their book.

"Put me down, Marchant."

The madman complied. He sat down breathing hard. Lois couldn't tell if the labored breath came from the exertion or the passion he felt.

"I know what this invention can do," he said. "And I will not, like Einstein or Nobel or a thousand others, allow my genius to be used for destruction."

Lois was standing over him. She put a hand on his shoulder. Through the heavy cloth of his blue shirt she could feel the electric excitation of his fervor.

"What can be done?" Lois asked.

Marchant looked at her. Even with him sitting and her on her feet they were almost the same height.

"We have to take charge of the dissemination of this tool. We have to guard the secret and pass it among the masses with caution and with guile."

"How do you see that playing out?" Lois asked. "I mean we don't have the resources of an InterCybernetics or the government."

"We need two things," Marchant said, "a sugar daddy and a host. You will provide both of those indispensable items."

"Why would I do this for you, Dr. Lewis?"

"Because you know that I'm right. You know that the world is filled with suit-and-tie-wearing Neanderthals who have no notion of beauty or peace or the harmony of humankind. You know that this invention of mine will be used to dominate and destroy if we don't take control."

SIX

LOIS REMEMBERED STARING at Lewis's huge face and thinking that he may have been right. Without physical experience, without time passing she had come to know his convoluted, half-insane musings. She was thinking, *He's crazy but he might not be wrong* as she walked down the hallway of the second floor of the house. What she answered to Lewis was forgotten or maybe she hadn't answered; maybe she just walked away from him lost in the dream of what he called the Co-mind.

Coming to a drab green door she knocked.

"Come in," the French-Arab girl called from the other side.

The room was a shock to Lois but not in the way that Marchant and the others had astonished her, from inside her mind. This was an external surprise. The room, approximately fifteen feet deep and twenty wide, was comprised of six massive acrylic paintings. The ceiling was a huge cavern dark in places but leading, somewhere far above, to a source of sunlight that illuminated much of the deep earth that was the subject. The style was hyper-realist and so there was no flat plane but a vastness that seemed to go on for thousands of feet.

The wall before her was a forest of small pines making up a primeval woodland that went on and on. Here and there on the ground there was evidence of a fire that had destroyed the older, larger trees to make way for new life. Lois wasn't certain but she believed that if she got close to the wall she would see insects and birds in flight and on the move.

The left wall was bisected nearly perfectly between a blazing sun next to which loomed the emptiness of black space. The star was so bright that Lois winced at its light. She stopped moving halfway into the room at the foot of the single mattress on the floor.

The right wall was almost a letdown; merely two galaxies colliding, their bulbous, dense cores of stars only just making contact. These too were surrounded by lightless space except in the lower left-hand corner where fat and naked Marchant Lewis flailed in the weightlessness of free fall. He was somehow connected to the immense nexus of stellar drama.

The closing door caused Lois to turn. Cosette, wearing a shapeless gray frock, was standing before a rendition of Javier's carnival. It was daytime and there were Mexicans of all ages and sizes and dark and light coloring wandering around the mechanical playground. The point of view was slightly elevated and so the whole of the carnival and the desert beyond was in perfect view. In the car at the top of the Ferris wheel Javier was kissing a Mexican girl who had Cosette's face.

Lois turned around slowly looking at all the paintings in turn. The corners were treated in such a fashion that one painting flowed into the other without the expected, jarring transition.

Then Lois looked down.

The world beneath her was a bird's-eye view of a vast mountain range a few hundred feet above the highest peak on the clearest of clear days. Acrophobia gripped Lois and Cosette rushed forward to grab her forearms. The mountainsides were lovely and fierce. Lois sat on the mattress and Cosette lowered with her.

"Why, why are you wearing clothes?" Lois asked the girl.

"I don't know. I knew you were coming to visit me and so I put this on. Do you wish me to take it off?"

"How long?" Lois replied.

"I don't know what you mean."

"How long did it take you to make these paintings?"

"Seven weeks. I work every day, every day. The walls I see go on forever and they cannot hold me in. I can climb into the ceiling or fall through the floor. Of course we can always travel in our minds to far-off places. But sometimes I just want to open my eyes."

"You are the most talented painter I have ever met," Lois said.

"It is not me."

"What do you mean?"

"Javier has the eyes of a painter. He sees into things and makes them through me."

"Does his room look like this?" Lois asked but she knew that it did not even as the words left her mouth.

"No. There is something in his brain, something that has nothing to do with painting but it stops him from taking the time. I did all this for him, from him."

Lois leaned forward and kissed Cosette on the lips. There was gratitude in her heart and she realized that the Javier in her was thanking Cosette for his expression through her.

"I don't understand," Lois said.

"That is because you are still thinking as one person who is alone in the cold embrace of uncaring, inert matter. You go to sleep alone and wake up that way. You walk alone even in crowds and you resent it when a man grabs you by the hair . . ."

Terry Pantalone grabbed her by the hair when they were making love three years before. He was a butcher for a big hotel in downtown San Francisco and when she was on top of him and he pulled her hair she felt something inside her and pulled away . . .

"It's okay, Lois," Cosette said. "We are together, have always been so. The problem is that we haven't had the luxury of loving each other as we do ourselves. Our senses are not up to it and our imaginations are filled with fear."

"I'm, so scared," Lois said. "Yesterday or the day before I was just a normal person walking around, feeling important. And today I realize that I was no more than a, than a bug. One of those bugs in that forest you painted, something I can't even see from here."

"We are," Cosette said and then paused. A moment later she continued. "We are all encompassing, everything and nothing at all. Our thoughts are ephemera but together they surpass the human animal and even the genome. We are the ground below the first step of ascendance."

"Is that you talking?" Lois asked.

"He is in me," she said. "The words are his but I understand them in a way that makes him like that picture on the wall. We are bugs in the grass on the ground before the stairway to godhood. We will never die even after we are lost and forgotten by the minds that rise from this fire."

"How can we know so much?" Lois asked. "I mean you and Javier and Frank and Marchant? It's more than any one mind can hold."

Instead of answering Cosette pounced at Lois hitting her in the upper part of the chest with the heels of both hands. Lois fell backward on the mattress and in the fall felt a shift in consciousness. Her back hit the ground instead of a soft cushion. She was looking up at a blue sky from a desert floor somewhere far away from Javier's carnival. And on her chest was a leering coyote, not Cosette.

The canine licked her face and batted its muzzle against her cheek. This was the *dog* that she'd seen in the shadowy hall that led to the kitchen. Lois tried to get up but the wild thing shifted to maintain its balance using its weight to keep her down. She tried to push at it but it snapped at her hand, not hard enough to draw blood.

Suddenly the beast leaped off of her and crouched down like a dog inviting play. She reached out for her but the coy moved out of reach and then jumped at Lois, knocking her down again. Instead of frightening her, the surprise brought a laugh to Lois's throat.

It was bright day in a limitless desert where no human being had ever been. Lois jumped suddenly and before the coy could prance away she caught it by a hind paw. It yanked and twisted and even though it broke her grip Lois had time to get to her feet managing to hug the creature around its skinny chest. She could feel the fast beating animal heart. The coyote bit her playfully and they rolled in the dirt; Lois laughing and the coyote yipping in glee.

As they rolled and tumbled, jumped and bit Lois began to experience strange sensations. The first was a sense of smell that had great range and a kind of, of language. Her new friend's rectum and teats had pungent and sweet scents while distant clouds smelled heavy with water. The desert around her shimmered as if seen through a crystal wall where, here and there, remote subjects—a cactus, a Gila-shaped stone, a patch of barren soil—would now and then come into hyper-clear focus.

And the music . . .

She could hear the blood throbbing in her playmate's throat and the winds, far above, shrieking their endless song. There was the sound of motes of dust pinging on stone and a hidden animal licking its tough hide.

Her own claws scratching across the baked ground vibrated in her paws and her ears. And her scent was strong, her name announced by her pelt and rectum and wet dripping maw.

The play fight got wilder and she was ecstatic with the

hint of blood and the taste of Cosette/coy. She felt a sudden pain, a bite too hard, and butted her head against her friend sending the overzealous coy rolling against a big rock.

For an instant there was a chance for real anger between them; the milky Cosette crouching down, and looking up at the beast that was once Lois. And then, in the periphery of both their keen eyes, there was a quick dash and Lois/coy and Cosette/coy were off, yellowy brown blurs after the desert hare that moved a moment too soon.

It was Lois/coy who caught the zigzagging creature by the scruff of its neck. She shook her head as she had many times before feeling the crack of bone and the blood seeping onto her tongue. There's a moment of grinning greed; the sun shining and the winds speaking her name. Then the tug from Cosette/coy and the playful tearing apart of the dead hare. Ripping the flesh and devouring it, licking the blood from the slick pelt and howling now and again.

Lois was rolling on her back when Cosette leaped up onto all fours and rushed away, her tail leaving her name on the air.

LOIS/COY SHOOK HER head and found herself following the scent of sweet milk. She loped along the hard desert floor sniggering at clouds and cacti and sand. She followed the odor of blood and friendship as they passed over and down, to the left and right, past scat and scorpions and sand. There were no thoughts in her mind, no idea of a thought beyond the snug feeling of her tight belly and the taste of hare flesh still on her tongue.

The spoor trail led to a large pile of flat red rocks standing out in the desert like a home for the weary. The taran-
tula and kangaroo rat, desert lark and roadrunner, seed
and cacti . . . and Cosette/coy with her brood of suckling
pups.

Lois/coy heard the canine growl and then yell before seeing Cosette/coy lying on her side with five babies sucking at
her milky teats. Lois/coy cowering and wanting to approach
her friend; remembering her own suckling puphood and
wanting to devour a babe or two.

Cosette/coy screamed a high-pitched warning and Lois
settled some distance away. Folding her paws and laying her
sleek head down, she watched as Cosette peered over the
bobbing heads of her pups.

The heat rose in the afternoon and Lois/coy drowsed.
The yips of the hungry pups lulled her and she no longer
had the desire to rip and rend. The coyote smells on the
breeze reminded her of a long history of traveling, traveling along nearly invisible trails that her kind had known for
thousands of years.

In her sleep her feet scuttled quickly out of the way of
the puma and the great black bear. She stalked fish in the
rivers where she drank and played with the porcupine that
never stabbed her even once.

Under a moon that seemed to take up the entire sky,
blazing in the cold cloud-ridden night, she migrated unable
to sleep more than a few hours at a time. Something called
to her, something dark and sonorous, something that she
ached for but did not know or understand.

She whimpered on the hotbed earth then Cosette/coy

licked her neck. Lois/coy got up gratefully pressing her
head against her friend. They licked each other and rolled
together. They whimpered in happiness at finding a friend
again.

They rolled and licked and inhaled each other's scent
until Lois opened her eyes. She was underneath Cosette
licking her labia, her chin slick with the Arab girl's discharge.
Cosette was at the other end doing the same to her.

Lois pushed and kicked Cosette away. She tried to get to
her feet but the orgasm weakened her legs and she fell toward the carnival door.

"*Arrête,*" Cosette said, reverting to French.

"I have to go," Lois replied fumbling at the painted door-
knob and stumbling into the hall.

SEVEN

IN HER ROOM again Lois sat on the high bed hugging her knees. She had never made love to another woman before. And Cosette wasn't even a woman. She was a teenager, a girl. But the satisfaction lingered, the sudden opening and flowing outward; the muscles that clenched hard around some place that she had never known even in her own private explorations.

But, while the guilt bore into her, she wondered about those coyotes and the desert that was so pure and vast and free from the plastic and asphalt and glass detritus of man.

Where had the child taken her? How?

This internal question coincided with a tapping at her door. It was a soft knock, feminine. Lois worried that it was Cosette come to drag her back to the desert to transform her again, to ravish her. Her heart beat with fear and anticipation. She did not move or make a sound.

The tapping came again, no louder.

Lois wondered if she could escape through the window.

She'd drive to Grant's place tell him that Marchant had drugged her and beg him to have her committed. In a straight-jacket in a cell under the influence of sense-deadening drugs she would begin to escape this nightmare. She would not feel anything, imagine anything.

"Lois?" a man's voice called—Frank.

"Go away," Lois said.

She went to the window. There was no fire escape, no trellis or even a ledge.

"Let me talk to you, Lois," the gambler said. "I know how disturbing all of this can be."

"Go away."

"I could no more do that than the gray goose could fly north in the winter."

Lois pressed up against the window frame with both hands. She expected it to be nailed shut but it went up with no problem. She was looking on the sunlit street but thinking about that goose; that solitary gray goose going the wrong way with no friends to help it, looking for something that was not there.

"Lois."

"What?"

"You need us."

"I don't even know you."

"Maybe not," Frank said. "Maybe you don't know us in the physical ways that you have known family and friends of the past. But this is a new day. We are beyond lunches and trysts and jokes about the current president. We have left behind hierarchies and schemes and one man, one vote. You feel it. You know it."

"I don't need you," Lois said.

"What will you do out there?" Frank asked as if he knew that Lois was standing at the window wondering how to get away.

Down on a patch of grass at the curb two young black children were playing a game that involved touching each other's shoulders. They were laughing and too near the traffic, in a world of their own but under the impotent gaze of the Korean-American science manager.

She turned and went to the door. It was unlocked. Frank could have walked in whenever he wanted.

He was wearing a yellow-green felt suit with a dark green hat that sported a red feather, and short white gloves that revealed his pale wrist. The thin mustache went well with his slender face. His green eyes seemed somehow appropriate for a gambler.

"What?" she asked, exasperated by the inanity of her quest to make sense of what was happening to her.

"May I come in?"

"Are you going to take me out of my body to some crazy place?"

Frank smiled and shook his head.

Lois backed away and he entered leaving the door wide open.

Frank sat on the oak floor in half-lotus. This surprised Lois. She had figured him for a chair and maybe a cigarette. She backed away perching at the edge of the high bed.

"Why do you think I need you?" she asked.

"Without us you will wander through this world having experiences and feelings that no one will understand. They will label you as weird or worse—insane. You will be in a thousand places you've never known, talking to people like me and Marchant and Marie."

"What did Cosette do to me?"

"I don't know. That was between the two of you. But what I can say is that whatever transpired that is not what you should be wondering about."

The gambler, for some reason, calmed Lois. It wasn't so much what he said but the demeanor he struck while addressing her. His gloves and silly hat allayed her fears. His sitting on the floor . . .

"What should I be asking?"

"Marchant is a monster," Frank said. "It is as if you were strolling around in the Muir Woods and then suddenly came upon a great *Tyrannosaurus rex*. He's a monster but he can't help it. He's hungry for you but he can't help that either. The world, our world is filled with monsters. Organized religion and nuclear power, indiscriminate sex and nationalism all kill with such regularity and in such awesome numbers that we are numbed by the crimes and blood and wars. But still we walk around the streets calmly as if our history wasn't a list of holocausts and annihilations."

"What's your last name?" Lois asked.

"Grimes."

"Where did you go to school, Frank Grimes?"

"No school. My father was a burglar and my mother was a part-time whore. I've been to more cities than a presidential candidate or the Fuller Brush man. The only thing I could read, before coming to this house, were racehorse names. The only math I got is counting cards—up to four decks."

"But you speak so eloquently. You all do."

"That's the monster in us," Frank said gazing down. "I can't read a word but I can recite Shakespeare. I couldn't do long division but I could explain why there is no absolute standard of length or time because of the theory of relativity. I am, we all are, part of the other. And if you run from us your mind will freeze up without the constant pruning of the Co-mind."

"What is the Co-mind?" Lois asked. She was so concentrated on his words that her insides felt invisible, intangible, inconsequential. Frank was knowledge and she was the vessel. This feeling elated her.

"The Co-mind, as Marchant says, is the nexus of the human soul and what lies beyond it. We are one soul throughout history, one continuous, riotous ramble from the caves of sub-Saharan Africa to the igloos of the Eskimos. Our languages living for centuries, our talents honed over the ages. We are more than simple small lives bumping around tiny quarters learning and forgetting at a furious pace through the briefest span of time. We have become each other and therefore we are forced to think as one and many."

"That's . . . that sounds crazy," Lois said.

"So would a jet plane to an ancient Hopi or a distant galaxy to Galileo. We, you and I, are the beginning of a new age . . . the age of the mind. At any moment you could enter my experience, feel my history, my sex. And I could know what you do. In some ways I might be able to do things that only you could know but only I could make real."

"Like Cosette painting what Javier sees."

"Yes," Frank said. "Marie's eyes are clearer than mine, her heart cares nothing for the rush of the game. And so she, through me in her, can play poker or blackjack better than I ever could."

"And you," Lois added, "are a better cook even though the talent is hers."

"We are one," Frank said, imploring Lois.

"That's crazy."

"Possibly," Frank said holding up his hands and gazing into the palms. "But our world would seem crazy to the ancients and that doesn't make us crazy, at least not necessarily. Change makes people afraid but we cannot escape the impact and the reorganization that change brings to our lives."

"But if what you say is true how can I even know that I'm talking to you?" Lois asked. "Maybe you're just Marchant. You sound like him."

"In the world you have entered, Lois, there is no you and me as in the old days. We are interdependent minds maintaining our identity but aware in ways far beyond any other being in the history of this planet. We have gone beyond the instincts of survival and procreation. Our beings are in many ways immortal and our destinies are as one."

Lois understood what the thin white man was saying. She saw in his eyes, heard in his words an intimacy and empathy that she'd never experienced. They were sharing something inside of each other all because she'd put her

hand in a silver box and felt phantom oil oozing between
her fingers. She experienced Marchant's infancy, Javier's
favorite moment of innocent young love, unrequited and
all the sweeter for it.

"When Cosette touched me we became coyotes," she
said, her stomach knotting over the sex they shared.

"Lana C," Frank said with a nod.

"Who's that?"

"A coyote that came down from the hills and Marchant
fed in his Garden of Eden. It took seven months to get the
creature's confidence. Then Marchant developed a Datascriber that was like a water bowl. Cosette put her hand in
one side while Lana C drank from the bowl . . . Now our
family has extended beyond the limits of mere human
thought. Lana has taken us on month-long treks through
the experience of the coyote. We see through her eyes and
smell-language. We experience a spectrum of excitation that
no human has known in eighty thousand years, if ever."

"It had sex with me."

"Cosette is a child of the streets of Marseilles, an urchin.
When Marchant and Marie brought her back from a conference in France we were happy to have a child among us.

"You see, Lois, we are all a part of the monster's collec-
tion. He is building the Co-mind brick by brick with each
of us. We are the prototype for a new world being, a world-
mind. There will be gamblers and orphans, scientists and
wild things . . ."

"But Cosette didn't use the Datascriber on me," Lois said.
"She just touched me and it was like I was in her mind."

"Once we've been calibrated to the Love Machine our

nervous systems develop a sensitivity of their own," Frank said, wincing. "Sometimes I'll be walking down the hall and I just brush up against someone and I'm thrown into their mood, we . . . connect. It's very disturbing. That's why I always wear rubberized long sleeves and acrylic gloves."

"But why me?" Lois asked.

"Marchant would never have chosen the coyote if Cosette had not urged him in his dreams. She wanted a pet, a wild thing. No one wanted Javier but me. I saw the artist in him, the real American in him. And you . . . You are certainly Marchant's choice. We can all feel his need for you. Marie has resisted. She loves Marchant. In her mind he is always a young boy pointing out secrets to his mother. But, as much as Marchant loves her, he needs something in you. He has a whole file cabinet filled with your pictures and discarded mail. The afternoon after you merged he came in singing. Our whole evening session was devoted to the singularity of your mind."

"I'm nothing more than bureaucrat with a Ph.D.," Lois said. "I don't have any special talents. I could never make it as a researcher or even a good research assistant. That's why I went into the business of managing researchers for InterCyb. I can speak to research scientists but I could never do what they do. I'm too, too mundane."

"Javier killed six people in a rival gang in L.A.," Frank said. "He was an assassin for a fledgling drug business in the barrio. But we didn't want him as an enforcer. He has the soul of an artist. Most of us, people of Earth, do not know our beauty, our truth, our ultimate destinies. Take you for instance."

"What do you know about me?" she asked, knowing full well the answer.

"You are wasting your life herding scientists for a company that treats science as a cash cow for the stockholders. Is that what you want?"

Even though she expected those exact words there was a concussion in the question that sounded in a distant part of Lois's mind. She heard it as if it were the demolition of a condemned building that had stood long past its allotted time. She thought that this image was an odd interpretation, not the way she imagined things at all.

But Frank was right. She didn't want to be a well-educated shepherd of superior beings, gathering their scat for household gizmos and role-playing computer games.

"Come with me, Lois." Frank was standing over her. She hadn't noticed that he'd stood and come up beside her.

"Where?"

"To the evening session."

That was when language overwhelmed her last defense. The words, "evening session," were there in her mind like a pair of old slippers or a favorite mug. They were a place and a time and destination that was so ingrained that it was like the thousand-year-old trails followed by Lana C; like her own ritual flossing and tooth care at the end of every evening, even after making love with the shy and reticent Grant Tillman.

EIGHT

THE NEXT THING she knew she was walking down a rickety stairway from the first floor to the basement. The cellar was like any other she had seen; rough-hewn tables and benches strewn with tools, piled with boxes, a stacked washer and dryer against a wall under a weak bulb.

There was a hall that led to another part of the underground chamber. Frank led her this way and she followed feeling familiarity in her senses and a strangeness in her conscious mind. It was dank down there and the light seemed to be filtered through green glass.

When they came to the white door the coyote was already there, waiting. As Frank used his key on the lock Lana C licked Lois's fingers and the self-professed shepherd of scientists scratched the creature behind her long and pointed ears.

The next set of stairs was dark all the way down with a pool of light at the distant base; a light that tried but failed to illuminate the journey down ward.

Lana C scampered ahead while Lois felt her way tentatively, afraid of missing a step and falling.

It was a long way, longer, she knew, than it looked to be.

Reaching the bottom at last, Lois sighed. She and Frank entered a small room that held a large whitewashed table around which sat all the members of the Marchant Lewis cult. The subbasement was like a bunker; like a secret held underneath another secret—locked away where no one could find it, or suspect it, or even imagine it. They all sat in chairs, even the coyote, and in front of each one was a Datascriber half the size of the one used to usurp her mind. The DS Machines (as she came to call them) were connected by a tangle of wires that crossed and jumbled in the center of the table.

There were two empty places. Frank went immediately to his chair and everyone turned to Lois expecting her to take her place.

"I have to know what's going on first," she said in answer to the unspoken request.

"This was a child pornographer's studio," Marchant rumbled. "They would bring children down here and exploit them for needs that came down from beasts. Frank knew about him and we came in on him one night . . ."

Lois could see clearly, and simultaneously from four separate points of view, the Family as they closed in on the pornographers. They were slender white men with short haircuts, wearing short-sleeved button-up dress shirts with no ties. One was working a small digital camera while the other was talking to a naked three-year-old boy who was sitting on a filthy mattress, crying.

Lois watched from Marie's and Frank's perspectives as Javier approached the men with his semiautomatic pistol. She gazed from their eyes while feeling the blood rush in the Mexican's veins. Then, for a moment, she saw a dark room with tiny Javier and two dark-skinned men raping him one day that was actually many days one summer twenty-five years before . . .

And then Marie was hustling the children (there were five of them tied together, in various states of undress and makeup) up the long dark staircase. But even as she was moving up the stairs she was also in the room while Javier shot the men in their legs and their arms, while he stood over them salivating like a coyote, while the men begged and whimpered and cried out for help in a basement that they had soundproofed so carefully.

"Are we going to be all right?" a little black girl asked at the top of the stairs. At seven she was eldest of them.

And while she asked her question Lois felt the paroxysm of rage rise like fever on Javier's skin. She wanted to turn away from the killing but could not close her eyes to the children's fear. She didn't understand how she could be watching both at once but she knew that to turn off one point of view would be to turn them all off.

She watched Javier killing the pornographers. She was Javier killing the pornographers. She hushed the children's fears and wept with them and wept for the murders and was sickened by the blood and wounds of the men. Javier had shot off their faces.

The pornographers were buried in a junkyard a few miles from Marchant's Garden of Eden. The children lived in a private orphanage six blocks from World's End. Marie went there every day. Even in the vision she was continually turning her back on Lois . . .

". . . come sit with us, Ms. Kim," Marchant was saying.

She was back in the room, the room where countless children had been raped and tortured, bartered and sometimes killed. She had killed the perverts. She had saved the children. She had run for weeks under the Coyote Moon with no care for human worries and no knowledge of death.

"Why?" she asked, her voice trembling.

"Because I need you," Marchant Lewis said.

For some reason Lois turned to Marie at the moment Marchant spoke. There was some anger but more loss in her eyes.

Lana C yipped and Lois felt a burp of laughter in her chest. An old coyote phrase, that had no literal translation, brought her to her chair because sometimes there was no escape from sun and wind or the rain and nightfall.

She placed her hand on the flat plate before her. Simultaneously five humans and one beast touched their own portals entering into Marchant's *world beyond the self.*

NINE

THEY WERE ALL sitting at the same whitewashed table but something was different. Time was not passing. Neither heat or cold or any other tactile sensation agitated at the edges of her senses. She was not breathing or fidgeting in the way she had done for all her twenty-nine years.

"Am I in your mind?" she asked Lewis.

He turned his head toward her but still the after image of him looking straight ahead remained.

"We are in the limbo between places," he said. "It is the genius of the Datascriber. It can hold our minds together and separately in a place that is not corporeal . . . the soul is like steam rising from the boiling pot of consciousness."

"And we are mingling?" Lois asked.

"Look at her," Marchant said swiveling his head, becoming hydralike as he did so. "Can you see as she saw when remembering that night we killed McCann and Pirelli?"

Marie's orbs opened wide and Frank's eyes became slits.

"She has the eyes of a housefly," Javier said.

The coyote howled like wolf and suddenly disappeared.

"Walk with me, Lois," Marchant said.

He stood up and walked through the table holding out both hands. She reached out for him and was then standing though she didn't have the sensations of movement or gravity.

"This way," Marchant said.

He gestured to a place behind her and the next thing she knew she had turned. For a moment she saw the pain in Marie's face and then she was alone with Marchant in the Garden at midday on the most beautiful day of any year—ever.

A robin landed on Marchant's shoulder. The big man smiled and she realized that they were no longer holding hands.

"Look at yourself from my eyes," Marchant said.

Instinctively Lois closed her eyes and when she opened them again she was Lewis looking out upon herself. She was standing there but it was not her, not exactly. She was more substantial than she looked in the mirror and the photographs and videos that Grant insisted on taking. Her eyes were more intelligent, her lips fuller.

Lois closed her eyes opening them from her perspective again.

"Is this how you look at yourselves?" she asked.

"Look around the garden," Marchant replied.

Lois saw that Marchant's garden was so large that you could not see the end to it. It went on and on flowering and teeming with birds and insects and, in the distance, larger animals that growled and shook the earth.

"This is your place," she said.

"Though we can share points of view one on one," Marchant said, "none of us, not even I, can see from multiple eyes at the same time. I brought you here because I felt we needed a bureaucrat to organize us. Someone that could see systems of production so that we could all work as a team rather than like a clan reenacting whatever our childhood dramas might have been. But now I see that your talents go much deeper than that."

"You were going to hire me?" Lois asked. She felt the accusatory question coming from her lips but inside she was cold, almost emotionless. The world she had been introduced to was larger than anything she could encompass with feelings.

"The Co-mind is beyond personal interest," Marchant said as if to validate her state of mind. "There is no wealth outside of our memories and there is no meaning greater than what we do to realize the potential in each other. Can you imagine the inventions I could have created if I had your ability to see from multiple viewpoints at once?"

"I could never do anything like that before tonight," Lois said.

"The Datascriber often shows us things about ourselves that we could not have known in solitary life. The Love Machine makes us whole."

"Love Machine?" Lois felt her soul drifting in the doctor's ideal garden, under the never-setting sun. It was as if she were fading from existence, as if life were a dream and now that the machine he made took her from her body she realized that it wasn't possible, who she was; like in the sleeping dream she'd have as a child when she'd be flying over a vast wheat field only to remember that she couldn't fly and now she would have to crash to earth.

"Love," Marchant said like a teacher, "the coming together of destined mates. Not the romantic drivel you hear in songs or the fearful question asked by a child. It is you coming together with thousands who need you and who are there to make you whole.

"Do you understand me, Lois?"

"I do but I don't care," she said. These words came easily from her. After an entire life of holding back her feelings, the truth now came out of her without affect or intention. She had expected this freedom to come with some feeling of joy but there was no élan, no feeling of relief.

"But this is it," Marchant argued. "This is the new world sought after for five thousand years. This is what the Christians and every other religion has been waiting for. Can't you understand that?"

"What do you want of me?" Lois said.

Marchant slumped down heavily. Behind him was Lois's orange piano bench.

"I've been waiting for you," he said, his gaze downcast, his words filled with the emotion of loss.

"I'm here."

Marchant looked up and she saw, again through his eyes, that she was taller than a basketball player, more substantial than a bear.

"I need you to bind us," Marchant said.

"Why? You are here in this house with your friends and pets and secrets."

"Why won't you let me into your soul, Lois?"

"Does the rapist ask his victim to love him too?" she asked realizing as she spoke that this really was how she felt; at least these feelings were in her body at the table.

"The need of the many is greater than the desires of the few," the dwindling black man said.

"So what?"

"You must submit to and create the new world order." Marchant's voice was getting smaller and higher. "Without it we will be less than the animals we slaughter for food."

These words appeared to her like a distant star cluster in the deepest black void of otherwise empty space. They were so far away and small and dim that her primary feeling was one of hopelessness. They might already be dead and even if she'd left five thousand years before she'd barely be any closer to them. Hope was a distant being; it was hardly a memory after all that time.

"Lois?"

"What, Marky?"

"You are abandoning the human race."

"Are you the human race, fat man?"

"I don't have to look like this," he said.

"But you will always be a monster to me."

"To you and everyone else," he said, sadly. "For my whole life I've been a monster, a demon. Too big for some, too smart for others, and too black for all the rest. I can see patterns where no one else can. I can see relationships where they don't exist except for me. I am the creature in the basement like those pornographers; a two-headed beast that does these things, who breaks the teacup, and spills the soup."

The distant stars in nothingness still shone impossibly far away but Lois was thinking about Marchant. Hadn't she pursued him? Hadn't she hoped to get rich off of his brilliance?

"But it's impossible," she said feeling more substantive than the Garden of Eden.

"No," the slouching scientist said. "Not if you join us. Not if you join with me."

"But we are already joined," Lois argued. "You don't need my physical body. You already have my mind."

"No," Marchant said in a voice that now seemed cold and drifting as she had been before. "The Datascriber initially can only bring the uppermost part of being into the minds of others. What is deep within you must be openly shared, given freely and without reservation. The deepest you is still you and not a part of our fledgling Co-mind, just like the deepest part of me is still a thing apart."

"But surely you, Doctor, would give freely," Lois said. "You want this abomination to succeed."

"Yes. You're right. I am the abomination . . . ," Marchant said. Lois could feel the pain of his life as an outsider always wanting to connect with people, to have friends, to laugh around a table with a family that looked to him as someone they loved and needed.

"What do you want, Marky?" Lois asked again.

"I cannot help who I am, Lois. I didn't know how to sit

down in a restaurant and coddle you. I didn't know how to
make you less afraid of me. There are people starving and
a planet being tortured; there are thousands of young men
and women at war and children with the eyes of old men.

"Lana C tells of us of a world that we have only begun to
understand. Not the canine world of biology but the spiritual vision of a place beyond ours. Javier creates beautiful
images in a cavern in his mind that rivals Michelangelo. Cosette can survive, at least in her mind, in the coldest, deepest
part of the ocean.

"I have been spit upon by people my entire life. My father will not speak to me. He's embarrassed by the way I
look and the way I acted as a child. I once applied to be a
translator in Asia but the host country's representatives
told me that they only hired white English teachers. I've
never been on a date I haven't paid for and even my teachers hated me.

"You hate me. And when I think about that I know
you're right. I don't fit in normal chairs or in family albums
or schoolrooms or even on the street. Even if I wasn't the
size of a hippopotamus . . ."

Lois *remembered* being young Marchant and being called
my little hippo by his father, Louis Lewis.

". . . I would still be the oddball, the Odd John. I was
arrested and held in jail for suspicion of murder for nine
days because the police said I looked suspicious . . ."

"Dr. Lewis," Lois said or thought or felt.

"What?" The man's words watery with real and imagined tears.

"It doesn't matter what pain you've felt, does it?"

"No. I guess not."

"What do you want of me?"

"I'm afraid to ask again."

"It's okay. I'm here now. You have me. And if the only way out is through your request let's get it over with."

"Bond with me," he said.

"I don't know what that means."

"I haven't hijacked your personality," he said. "I've shown you the entrance to a world of extraordinary beauty and grace. You haven't entered. You haven't become a part of us. And without you there may well be no tomorrow."

"Hyperbole, Doctor," Lois said from a place that had rarely shown itself in public; a place of pure intellect and nearly absolute disdain.

"No," Lewis said. "No. We need your vision and I need you to understand me."

"But why?"

"Bond with me and you will know."

"I trusted you with the Datascriber and now I'm a car thief and lost in a world where I don't know what's real and what is not."

"What was real, Gooseberry?" Marchant Lewis asked. "Your daily life with a green sports car and that beautiful but reticent boyfriend or the sorrow you feel every night before falling asleep?"

"I thought you hadn't gone deeply into my mind, Doctor?"

"I haven't. These feelings of yours are right out on the surface like a, like a blistering sunburn. Your depths are beyond me."

His words unveiled an imagined month-long dialogue between best friends. It was as if they had come together after some disaster and there they began to share secrets while foraging for food and praying for deliverance.

She was sad every night before falling asleep, even when Grant was snuggled up at her side. Her job meant nothing to her. It was only there so that she could tell her parents that she was well-off while looking for a husband; a good Korean husband like her father—silent and strong, tenacious but civil. She left home every morning, boarded a plane six times a month to visit her scientists. She collected jazz CDs but rarely listened to them anymore. And every day she could make the time she went to the movies alone and sat in an aisle seat, at the back row, eating popcorn and imagining that she was one of the background characters—watching life from up close.

It started in middle school when her mother punished her for bringing home a single B among a report card otherwise filled with As.

"You cannot see your friends, watch TV, or go to the movies until your next report," her mother, June Kim, had told her.

There was never any wiggle room with June. Her father, Kenneth Kim, would not override June's decisions in the home.

"She is your mother," he would say simply and with finality.

That night her grandfather died in his small apartment. His hotplate had set fire to the muslin curtains. They found him in his bed burned black.

She heard a child laughing then and ran down a path in Marchant Lewis's garden.

She came to a greenish porcelain fountain. Leaves and dirt covered the bottom of the waterless bowl. Little sparrows were rubbing their feathers in the loose dirt, wallowing and singing merrily as if Lois were not there.

Laughter pealed again and Lois went past the dry pond and its frolicking birds. She ran into the bushes. On the other side she saw herself at the age of twelve running with three girlfriends and laughing, laughing. It came to her that she hadn't laughed with abandon since her grandfather died—the last day she ever got a grade less than an A.

She had given up her laughter and gained perfection, her mother's ideal. The trade seemed so obvious; the forces at play so clear. They were poor and good grades would buy her and her parents an easier life. And life was easy. One day blended into the next like mild, meaningless waves meandering across a profound ocean only to come up onto the shore where they ceased to exist.

The children were still laughing. Little Lois fell and hurt herself but the next moment she was up and running again, playing with her friends.

Her child's self was like the splash made by some diver in that ocean; going down deep to a place where her mother had never been.

"Lois."

Marchant was still there beside her, though she had run pretty far, she was sure. The big black outcast reached out to her.

Lois didn't move. Instead she looked at his hand thinking of how he had violated her. Moving his mind into hers, no matter how far the invasion went, was an evil thing, a terrible thing.

At the same time she was thinking from the heart of the child that still knew how to laugh out loud.

"Can I be free of you?" she asked.

Marchant stared at her for a long moment. In that time Lois noticed that high clouds were hurrying across the sky. She wondered, idly, if this was not a sign of their creator thinking.

"Yes," he said at last.

"I can get the gambler, the urchin, the lame science student, and the gangbanger out of my head?" At each term she stopped and took in the full image of the cult member.

Marchant nodded sadly.

"What about you and the dog?" she asked.

"All gone, Lois. All gone. All you have to do is say the word. The Datascriber can reverse its initial affects."

"Will I stay in your minds?"

"What little it is we have of you."

Transported again Lois was in her house on a Saturday when her mother was gone all day to wash clothes, do her shopping, and go to her cousin's house to play cards. All day long Ken Kim moved in silence, reading the Korean newspaper, fixing the plumbing, or just sitting in his chair staring off into space while smoking Pall Mall cigarettes.

Lois would watch him from behind corners, quiet as falling dust. She wondered if he thought that he was completely alone what he might do. She noted every time he scratched or stood up, when he got water or went to the toilet. She was waiting there, hidden behind his silence.

And in Dr. Lewis's imagined garden she was just as quiet and concentrated. When she was a child she wanted to come out from the shadows and shout, "Boo!" just to get a rise out of her father. In the garden place, with children laughing in the distance, she wanted her freedom but could not utter the words to demand it.

Finally she sighed and reached out for the behemoth's fat fingers.

TEN

THE TRANSITION WAS instantaneous and absolute. The child-sized woman and the bearlike man were standing on air a few feet above the ocean. There was no land in sight. The sun was hot and they, Lois and Lewis, were naked. His fat belly hung down but his penis was so large that it lolled even lower making his middle section reminiscent of a dark elephant with the hollow navel making its one blind eye.

"Is this another place you go?" she asked him.

"No, Lois. We are in your mind now."

"I have never thought about a place like this before," she said but on the crest of her consciousness was the metaphor of the mild waves that stood for her wasted days.

"See me, Lois," Marchant Lewis said.

"What does that mean?" she asked.

"I am as I am before you," he said as if reciting a sermon given by a traveling preacher. "I have never fit in the world but I hold its future in my mind."

Reaching forth Lois placed her hands on the big nude belly. His tight skin, or the image of his skin, was hot to the touch but not uncomfortable. He felt like a stone that absorbed solar heat on a cloudless winter day. She luxuriated in the warmth. And then her hands began to merge with his flesh; below the dermis into a thick layer of fat. It wasn't like her hands passing through water but more like cold air colliding with warm. The feeling frightened her but the ecstasy she felt canceled out this fear. She entered through his abdomen becoming him as she climbed. Never had Lois felt so connected to anything, not even her own thoughts, not even the orgasm she felt with Cosette.

She moved in up to her shoulders and then allowed her head to enter the obese misfit. Sight and sound and smell all receded into one great sense organ that brought information to her mind in a completely new way. Knowledge had weight, laughter rhymed with color, the scent of her grandfather told his every tale.

When Lois had entered Marchant completely he bellowed in a tone so deep that she could feel the pain of her invasion. He tried to move away but she was inside him now, a part of him. Together they fell into the ocean sinking slowly below the inconsequential ripples. Marchant beat upon his own chest and Lois spread out her arms to embrace him from inside. He tried to stop breathing and she swam into his lower brain calling on his lungs and heart and mind to continue on their lifelong journeys.

"We're drowning," he said to drive her out.

"We can survive anywhere," she replied while opening the places that he had hidden even from his mother.

"I was wrong," he said.

"You are mine," she answered.

"I didn't know that it would feel like this," he cried.

"Submit to me, Marchant Lois," she said.

Her poetry distracted him from his fears. Combining their names calmed him enough to become catatonic for a moment.

. . . AND THEN THEY were children, in a long-ago past, naked, atop a huge black mastodon trudging with purpose toward a distant cloud of dust.

Marchant, afraid of falling, hugged Lois from behind. And she leaned forward to see what the prehistoric pachyderm was headed for.

"I'm afraid," Little Marky cried.

"You were the one who wanted to come here," Lois said in her most serious child voice.

"But I don't wanna."

In the distance Lois began to make out a vast herd of mastodons. She could hear the thunder of their march and feel the straining of the beast beneath her to reach her family.

"We have to," she said.

"Why?" he whispered at the back of her neck.

The question and his breath on her neck exhilarated Lois. She turned to the fat boy and wrapped her arms around him. They merged once again and he swooned from the pressure.

"It hurts," he cried.

"That's why I'm here," she said.

"To hurt me?"

"No, silly, to help you get through the pain and to get all the way out there where your dream is."

"What dream?"

"The black mastodon's dream."

And then, as one, they were in the middle of the herd of thousands of the extinct creatures. They cried and bellowed and thundered through life not as single entities but as the mind of the many on a journey that was endless. Beneath their feet lay the bones of thousands more that had died on that path. They crushed these bones into dust, which became the firmament of their passage.

"Oh my God," said Marchant Lewis.

Lois knew that this was the first time he had evoked the name of the deity.

They were on the back of the mastodon, Lewis holding on to Lois for his life.

"I will be your beast of burden," she said. "I will carry you to that far-off destination."

"I've been waiting for you," he said. "It feels like forever."

"I hate you for what you've done to me," she replied. "But life cannot make those distinctions."

"I'm sorry," Marchant Lewis said.

"I know."

"I would have done better if I could have."

They were in the ocean again.

"I know," she said. "I hate you but I have forgiven you too."

He was hovering above the ocean again, the small waves

merging like the days of a meaningless life below him.

"I can't ask for more," Marchant said.

"But what happened?" she said as she crawled out of his broad abdomen.

The easement of pressure felt like an unending discharge, like bleeding out the last drop of an infection.

"It will take years for us to know that, my dear Gooseberry."

They drifted in the air above the ocean that went from horizon to horizon.

"Marchant Lois," they said in unison.

Slowly he sank into the sea.

For a very long time Lois floated in place wondering what had happened. Their minds, she knew, had come together as one and therefore their thoughts were shared symbols and images, metaphors and lost dreams. Everything meant something. The pachyderms and pachyderm bones, the smell of dung and the dust they raised in their wake. There were images that were not clear at the time: insects and sores, huge mastodon erections and a female at the head of the pack leading them on and at the same time being pressed by the surging masses at her back.

"Marchant?" she said, wishing to discuss what she now realized.

But he was gone. He had sunk to the bottom of the ocean and even now he was being devoured by sea-bottom crabs and shrimp. Lois could see him there, his face expressionless, his fat nearly weightless in the heavy pressure of the lower regions.

ELEVEN

SHE OPENED HER eyes even though they seemed to already be open. Across the table from her Marchant Lewis had slumped forward, his head hanging midair as his fat belly kept it from coming to rest on the table.

Marie was already on her feet hurrying to the fat man's side. Most of the others were rising. Only Lois and Lana C remained motionless. Lois stared at Marchant while the coyote gazed at her.

Marie touched Marchant's shoulder lightly but this was enough to knock him over. He fell to the floor soundlessly— dead.

Lois watched as the doctor's people gathered around him, laying their hands on him.

"What's wrong?" she asked, many questions aligning themselves in those two words.

"You killed him," Marie accused.

Lois understood the lame student's passion but the words made no progress in her mind.

Cosette cradled Marchant's huge head in her lap.

"He wanted me to merge with him," Lois said feeling that her words were redundant, unnecessary. After all everyone at that table had witnessed the interplay between the scientist and his personally appointed warden. They knew about the laughing children and the dusty birds. They knew about the huge mastodon and Marchant's big limp cock.

"He was to have a triple bypass Thursday next," Frank Grimes said. He was down on one knee behind Javier. The young banger pressed both of his Jesus tattooed palms against Marchant's chest.

"They said that his chance at survival was six out of ten," the Mexican said.

Lois found that she already knew all this. Marchant had tried to merge with everyone in that room, even the coyote. He had various levels of success but never was he able to transfer a viable, full version of himself into the mind, no—the soul, of another. Each one of them had a piece of the madman in them but no one could take all of his plans and machinations.

There was little time left. Marchant had an inkling, when he first used the Datascriber on Lois, that she was his possible soul mate.

"He died for you," Cosette said.

"He used me," Lois replied. "He didn't want to die and so he used me like a garage. He parked his big fat ass in my head."

"He loved you," Frank Grimes said, pain in each word. "He loves you."

"Like a coyote loves blood," Lois replied. "Like a queen bee loves her drones."

"You aren't worthy of him," Marie said. Pressing against the half-exposed belly she got to her feet. "I should kill you."

"But you won't, Tiny Dancer," Lois said unable to keep the sneer out of her tone. "Will you?"

The shock on Marie's face gave Lois an unpleasant rush of satisfaction. It was the feeling she had astride that mastodon; a feeling of power where there had been none before.

"I'm tired," Lois said. "I'm going up to my room. Everyone meet me down here tomorrow afternoon at two. That's when we start."

"What do we do with the body?" Javier asked.

"Bury it in the garden and plant potatoes over it."

"It?" Marie uttered. She leaped at Lois but Frank caught her and held her back. Lana C put herself between the sputtering Marie and Lois. The coyote bared her fangs but did not growl.

THE CANINE ACCOMPANIED Lois from the subbasement to her second floor door. When Lois went in the once-feral bitch curled up in the hall, the self-assigned sentry to the new master of the cult.

Inside Lois closed the door and reached for the lamp.

"Leave the light off, Gooseberry."

He was sitting on an orange piano bench across from her bed. He seemed smaller now, more manageable.

"I thought you were in my head?" she said, making sure not to sound frightened or surprised.

"You don't have to be so cruel, Lois. You have the power now. Lana C is the barometer for alpha dominance among us."

"What do you want now, Marchant?"

"I have everything I need. My soul passed into your keeping as life fled my body. I felt myself dying as you offered me safe harbor."

"I can't let go of hating you," she said in even tones.

"That is of little importance. You can torture me or ignore me or just make me listen to opera. I hate opera. Anything you wish to hand out I must accept. I'm free of the body in the world of the mind. And now I have you to bear me, to carry out my plan."

"What plan? All you know is that you want to conquer the world. That's not a plan. That's a dream or a nightmare, a paranoid fantasy."

"You know better, child. You have traveled the desert with the beast, seen the arid beauty of primal being. You know that everyone you've ever known has lived only a half-life at best. You know that one moment in my psyche has evolved you past all the fast foods and sitcoms and people wanting to lead you."

"I didn't ask for that knowledge."

"Greatness doesn't knock," Lewis said. "It breaks down the door and grabs you by the throat."

Lois wanted to deny him, to make him, and his phantom bench, disappear but she knew these desires were futile and wrong. They were one being, not two. His invasion of her mind had brought her to consciousness for the first time in her life. There was no escape. There was no other choice.

"What are we going to do, Marchant?" she said. The resentment and rebelliousness closed behind a door of necessity and truth.

"It was fate not malice that brought me to you, Lois," he said. "You *do* understand that?"

"How can we take over the world with no plan?"

"You will come up with the plan, child. And with me at your side there is no mind on Earth that can resist us."

ANYONE LOOKING FROM the outside would have seen Lois sitting on the edge of her bed talking to an empty wall. In the garden four cult members were digging a grave, then lowering five hundred and twenty-seven pounds of flesh therein. The coyote sat at the door listening for danger and between them all, in discrete sections, the architecture of a sundered world was forming like a salt crystals in a jet-black cave.

JUST BEFORE SUNRISE Lois lay back, still fully dressed, and fell asleep. In her dreams she knew that before she died all the nations and religions and belief systems of the world would have fallen before her like leaves in an autumnal windstorm.

She smiled in her sleep. But it was not the gentle smile her grandfather had known. Nor was it the mirth of that little girl. Her mind was filled with the obsessions of the huge black scientist. She was him, could be nothing else; she wanted nothing else.

TWELVE

Two weeks later Lois was sitting at the head of the meeting table on her orange bench in the subbasement with Lana C curled at her feet and the apparition of Marchant Lewis at her side.

"They'll be here soon," Marchant said in her mind.

"I know that."

"Are you ready?"

"Does it matter?"

"You must accept your role, Lois," the ghost said. "We are the instruments of history. We don't have the luxury of averting our eyes while the bombs fall and the wars wage."

They were speaking Spanish. For the past week Javier's tongue had passed between them as easily as if they had been raised in Mexico City.

Lana C licked Lois's fingers.

She closed her eyes only to open them on a scene of her grandparents working on their little farm near the mountains. She could hear them speaking in Korean. They labored over the makeshift grave of the soldier that came to them.

"He died for his country," Marchant said.

"Can't I have a moment alone even in my own mind?" she asked.

"We are the new nation, Lois. We must take action."

Turning to her left, away from Marchant, she was on the surface of the moon. It was chilly and illuminated by radiance rather than light. There was almost no atmosphere and so everything seemed crystal clear to her. She could have grown to the size of a gas giant and used the moon as a Ping-Pong ball.

"We are not gods but servants," Marchant said. "Our destiny is to serve."

Lois opened her eyes again and she was in the subbasement. A long-legged spider was prancing across the table, the digital clock upon the wall registered 16:03, and Marchant Lewis stood next to her wearing a herringbone jacket and cobalt-blue pants.

"You're losing weight," she told him.

"I am what you make me," he said, bowing his head.

On the second night after he'd died Lois had Marchant lashed to a torture table. There she beat his flesh with a thorny stick while fire ants crawled on him, slowly devouring his flesh. The ghost of Lana C entered the room and curled up in a corner, watching her masters and refusing to leave. Lois felt sexually aroused. She couldn't tell if it was the pain she was inflicting or the desire to be with the canine that affected her.

"You're the one who brought me here," Lois said in the subbasement.

"You're the one who stayed."

THE DOOR FLEW OPEN. Frank and Javier pushed a man with a black bag pulled over his head into the room. The man's hands were manacled in front of him. There was a noose around his neck and he was making meaningless, desperate sounds. His ankles were manacled together. He would have fallen if the men hadn't held him upright.

"Put him in the chair," Lois said.

When the man heard her voice he stopped struggling and went completely silent.

Frank and Javier pressed him down into an iron chair. They linked his feet to the front legs of the chair and ran a chain through the left cuff on his wrist to his left foot. Leaving his right hand free they pulled off the hood. There was electrical tape across his mouth; this they ripped off.

His left eye was swollen shut and an apricot-sized knot on his left temple was purple and bleeding slightly. The right side of his jaw was puffed up and bloated. Blood seeped from his lower lip.

Grant Tillman was not a handsome man that night.

Seeing him in this way saddened Lois. She regretted what she had done to him but realized that she had contempt for him also; his manly posturing and small dick; his privileged upbringing and the small tips he left at the finest restaurants in the Bay Area.

"Lois!" he cried. "Help me!"

"You can leave us," she said to the kidnappers.

Without a word Frank and Javier left the room, closing the door behind them. The coyote followed them. The digital clock read 16:12.

"Lois!"

"Hello, Grant."

"What's going on here, baby?"

"I'm really sorry about this," she said. "It's just that you were the best choice. The one we could investigate most fully."

"What are you talking about?" Grant said, flailing his free hand about. "Did you send those guys after me?"

"Yes," Lois said in a passionless tone. "I'm sorry. There was no other way."

"Are you insane? The police will come here. They'll arrest you for kidnapping."

"Put your hand on the metal disk in front of you, Grant."

"Let me go!" he jumped around as well as he could with one arm and both feet shackled to the chair. The chair was bolted to the floor and so Lois wasn't afraid that he'd fall over. And the Datascriber disk was glued to the tabletop, his only choice was to obey her request.

But not before he screamed.

If she had been in another room it would have been hard for her to tell if it was a man or a woman shrieking. The voice was high and very afraid. He juddered around and cried out from 16:13 to 16:16; then he slumped down in his bonds.

"Put your hand on the metal disk and I will let you go," she said.

"Lois," he pleaded.

In response she put her hand on the identical disk before her.

"Please," he rasped through a torn larynx.

"Your hand."

He's like a drowning man, Marchant whispered in her ear. *You are throwing him a lifeline.*

"Why are you doing this to me?" Grant said.

"I will call Frank and Javier back to make you place your hand there," she replied.

"I loved you," Grant begged.

"Put your hand on the disk or I will have them come back and beat you until you submit."

The pain in her lover's face pricked Lois. It brought to mind pictures of their tepid love affair like memories of a canceled TV show seen in the previous season.

What was the star's name?

He brought his hand slowly to the Datascriber plate.

It was 16:19.

He laid the hand down, splaying out his fingers.

The room shifted into another place disturbingly similar to where he'd been shackled. The only difference was that the chains were gone and a huge black man in sporty clothes stood there next to Lois.

"Where'd you come from?" Grant asked Marchant.

The dead scientist hunched his shoulders.

Realizing that his bonds were gone Grant leaped to his

feet and rushed Marchant. The big man grabbed the younger one by the shoulders.

"Sit down, Grant," both Lois and Lewis said together.

Every scintilla of his strength cried out to destroy the big black. He could feel the man's throat in his hands. But he found himself sitting in the chair, squirming and gurgling his hatred and desire to destroy.

"Calm yourself," the Co-mind said to its newest member.

Somewhere else another Marchant was giggling.

Grant felt the anger and rage flow out of him.

"How did you do that?" he asked. "Which one of you is talking?"

"Look at me," Lois said as Marchant took a step backward, half disappearing into the wall. "We are planning to conquer the world."

"The world? Are you crazy?"

"No. With this machine we are able to bring people's minds together. We can organize in complete secrecy and infiltrate, in minutes, any place or people or sect. We can gut a man or woman of their secrets in seconds."

"How?"

"Stand up and pull down your pants and underwear," Lois replied.

Grant did as he was told without physical hesitation. There was embarrassment and humiliation but it resided in some other space.

"You see?" Lois said.

Grant gasped at the size of his member. It was normal at least—maybe even larger.

"How?" he asked, looking up at her.

At that moment she looked away and the room shifted back again. Grant found himself shackled once more and free from the mental bondage of the metal plate.

A crash sounded behind him.

"On the floor!" a man's voice commanded.

Lois put her hands above her head.

"On the floor!" The shout was more urgent.

Lois stood up with her hands in the air. She seemed confident and unflustered to Grant. Three policemen in riot gear came into view. One grabbed Lois, pushing her to the ground violently.

Grant looked down at his pants expecting them to be down around his knees. But it was all a dream or a vision or . . . something.

The police were screaming at Lois, demanding that she give them the keys to Grant's bonds. He looked around for the huge black man. He was nowhere to be seen. But Grant could see no other door, no exit for the man to have used to escape.

THIRTEEN

"*You're gonna go* away for a long, long time," said Theodore Astor, the detective in charge of the Tillman kidnapping case. "We got you on everything from murder to kidnapping, from keeping a wild animal without a license to contributing to the delinquency of a minor."

At first Lois had been held in a cell with thirteen other women. She'd had three fights but didn't remember any of them. The coyote and Javier conducted her actions then. All she remembered were the guards pulling her off the women who had attacked her. In the last fight Lois had bitten off her opponent's ear. The blood, she remembered, made her hungry. After the last altercation she had been kept isolated from the general population.

"Are you listening to me, Ms. Kim?"

"I haven't killed anyone. I haven't kidnapped anyone," Lois said. "And as far as the other charges—the coyote you blame me for harboring eluded your officers and Cosette was already living in the house when I got there."

Astor would have been handsome if his face wasn't red-dened by broken blood vessels on his cheeks and nose. His eyes hadn't made up their mind whether they would be green or gray or both. His hands were powerful and blunt *but nothing compared to the size of Marchant Lewis's hands.*

"What about the corpse under the potato patch?" the detective asked.

"In the safe in his room Marchant left a letter saying that when he died he was to be buried in his garden. It also stipulates that his property would be left to his personal foundation and that I am to be the executor."

"Not if you murdered him."

"Your coroner will find that he had a heart attack."

"And Grant Tillman?"

"It was a joke that got out of hand," Lois said. "He will tell you that if you ever ask him."

"His parents have him in a mental ward. You drove him mad with the torture."

"He will corroborate what I say. I wanted to excite our sex life by having him brought to me like that. He knew about it but Frank and Javier must have scared him. They fought back in self-defense."

"Do you expect me to believe this horseshit?"

Lois smiled and closed her eyes simultaneously opening them on an endless shoreline. Marchant was standing under the shade of a palm tree looking at her. He was smiling, fading into darkness like the Cheshire Cat. Grant was seated at the waterline looking into the distance and into himself at the same time.

"So you think that you're going to walk out of here scot-free?"

"You have no idea what I'm thinking, Detective Astor," Marchant Lewis said through Lois's lips. "If you did you wouldn't be able to sleep for a month of Sundays and you would kiss your children every time you saw them. You'd go back to church and beg your God for forgiveness. I am beyond you and your crimes. I don't need lawyers or police-men, judges or congressmen. I am a law unto my selves and sooner or later you will bow to us."

Lois couldn't read the emotion on Astor's face and Lewis didn't care. They sat together in the metal frame chair, bound as Grant had been; chained because Lois was deemed dangerous after her fights in the communal cell. Now they kept her in a padded room and used five guards to shackle her before bringing her anywhere.

"Do you want a lawyer?" Astor asked, sidestepping the crazy talk.

"When the time is right."

"The public defender can appoint one."

"Grant will bring me a lawyer," she said. "He will de-fend me. He will tell you that it was all a joke, that Javier and Frank are innocent."

"You tryin' to get a section eight?"

"She is too young to understand your reference, Detec-tive," Lewis uttered through the young woman.

"She?"

"Can I go to my cell now?"

ALONE IN HER CELL, with Marchant off somewhere in the tropical forest and most of the others redefining themselves in her mind, Lois sat in the sand with the coyote at her side wondering how she got there.

Much of her mind was defined by intricate patterns rather than straightforward thoughts and the rest were metaphors in the sky and sand and sea.

Can I be me? the sky wondered.

Have I been sundered by the might of his mind? the sea hissed.

Lana C pressed her muzzle against Lois's ear making the human giggle. She stood up and walked out onto the ocean, the soles of her feet barely sinking into the water. She could feel the cold between her toes knowing that she couldn't sink; that this was her world as once God had called up a universe.

This thought made her wonder.

She loped back to the shore and picked up a branch that she knew would be there. With this piece of driftwood she drew an outline of a man. Using Javier's great skill she created the two dimensional form perfectly anatomically correct. Then she fell to her knees in the moist sand and began caressing first his face and then his chest and on down. As her hands moved what came to be known as the Intention traveled through them. A face appeared and a form that was both strong and lithe. His sex was ample but not overly large; his legs could run for great distances. His fingers were long, a pianist's hands, and he was smiling, a fully made man sunk in a perfectly fitted hole on the shore of an infinite beach in a land that had no name.

"Orrin." The name came to Lois's lips from somewhere deep inside her psyche.

She understood at that moment this world was perfect because it was a product of her unconscious mind; that this man was perfect because he was what she had wanted long ago. He was olive colored and not wholly Asian or Negroid or Caucasian. He resembled the man that had died on her grandparents' farm during the war. So he was an American.

"Lois," he said.

"Yes."

She was naked and he was on top of her, inside of her, hovering above and slowly entering then withdrawing, kissing her neck softly and saying her name.

The orgasm grew slowly, slowly. His breath smelled like a teacher she once had in the third grade. His skin was both taut and supple and his movements were designed to drive her crazy.

When she finally came it was with wild abandon. Her heart felt as if it might burst and her muscles ached with cramps from her desire to crush him to her and to run. When it was over she juddered, vibrating violently. As the intensity began to abate he leaned over as if to kiss her ear and whispered, "Again."

"No. Too much," she said. She could feel his erection hardening and the muscles tensing. His breath was coming faster and for a moment she considered turning him back into sand.

"You can't do that, Lois," he whispered. "It will isolate you from your own mind. It will make you into a rock."

The passions flowed again and Lois gave up to them. She

had never been so satisfied or so loved, so helpless and overpowered.

She fell asleep and when she awoke Orrin was gone. She saw his footsteps in the sand disappearing into the bank of trees where Marchant was no doubt watching.

The sun was setting. Lois sat up and wondered about all the people and strange creatures that she might create. *The mortal goddess,* she mused. And could Marchant and Frank and even Lana C create people, places, and other creatures inside her mind?

"I am the universe," she pronounced, "but still there are laws and urges to govern me."

The sky jostled and Lois opened her eyes upon five guards in full riot gear. She smiled and rose to her feet sated by Orrin's lovemaking and astounded by the fact that Lewis's Datascriber had started the creation of a whole new universe.

The guards shackled her hands and feet and the chains on her hands to the chains on her feet. Then they guided her to an interrogation room where a young white woman in sharp business attire and Grant Tillman awaited her. Lois was guided to a chair and chained to that chair. She accepted this treatment with equanimity. She was a huge black man in a slight Asian frame, a gangbanger from the barrio who expressed himself through the heart of a French-Arab urchin child. She wasn't even human and, as the people around her slowly, necessarily came to notice her abilities, how could they not fear her?

Grant had lost weight, twenty pounds at least. His skin was pale and his eyes haunted. He stared at Lois as, for the first time, a child sees his mother's extraordinary countenance.

Lois smiled for him. She gazed deeply into his hurt eyes and shook her head in admiration for his survival. She knew, from the Grant inside her mind, that this transition would be the hardest on the young white man. In order to become part of the Co-mind one had to submit to it. White men in general, and Grant in particular, saw submission as a weakness and so fought it beyond the limits of their ability to strive.

From talking to him in her own mind, in the cell in which she was held, Lois learned that her own submission was a strength. She learned from Marchant Lewis that carrying the load demanded by others built endurance and even a kind of genius.

And so she stared into Grant's eyes exuding empathy for his internal struggles. The police thought that the pain Grant felt came from the kidnapping but really it arose from the internal struggle the millionaire put up against the will of Marchant and Lois. There was a chance that he would die from the desire to be free of the will of others.

"Are you listening to me, Ms. Kim?" the woman was saying.

Do not let this woman touch you, Marchant said in Lois's mind. *There's something wrong with her. She is not for the Co-mind.*

"Excuse me," Lois said a little confused by Lewis's frightened tone. "What is your name?"

"I already told you."

"I wasn't listening."

"I'm Grant's lawyer, Jenna Urdé."

"Oh. And are you some fancy high-priced lawyer?"

Jenna smiled in a predatory manner.

"I usually charge a great deal of money for my services but after hearing the medical reports I offered to represent Grant gratis.

"I advised him against this meeting but he told me that if I didn't come he'd bring in another lawyer. I am here to represent his interests."

"And I am here," Lois said, "in here, to represent the interests of an entire world."

Jenna stared at Lois with deep interest. The lawyer had lustrous brown hair and olive-colored eyes. She was beautiful and bright. Lois found herself wanting to merge with her. She imagined them on the sand, on her beach, maybe with Orrin naked and compliant, for a change.

No, Marchant said. He was standing behind her, his ghostly hands on her shoulders.

Why not? she asked in her mind.

We are not slavers or ravagers, not seducers. We have a job to do, a purpose to achieve. You are the fulcrum of the Co-mind and in that position you must be above the hunger in your belly.

Who is the master? Lois asked the ether.

I am the fount not the captain or the overseer. From my mind comes the stuff of our project. Do not, Gooseberry, turn water into chains.

These last words reverberated in Lois's mind. She realized

that she loved Marchant, that he was the life preserver she had come upon almost by mistake floating in the wreckage of the modern world.

But you told me not to touch her, Lois mused. *You said that even before my fantasies appeared.*

She is dangerous, Marchant replied. *There is something wrong with the way she holds herself, her eyes . . .*

"Ms. Kim!" Jenna Urdé said.

"Grant, have you come to help me?" Lois responded.

"Y-yes."

"Have you told them that the kidnapping was a joke?"

"I have."

"Have you found a suitable property for our pod?"

"In Arizona. There was a small community development project there that fell prey to the real estate crash. If you have Marchant's money I will add mine and we'll be able to start our own community there. We'll be able to expand to a population of fifty thousand in five years."

"What are you talking about?" Jenna Urdé asked.

"Have you told her that she will be representing me?" Lois asked Grant.

"She knows."

FOURTEEN

SIX MONTHS LATER 117 adults had purchased 612 houses in World's End, the name they gave to a failed real estate development, on the outskirts of suburban Phoenix. This consortium of property investors all had one thing in common: their houses were connected by a private fiber-optic network and they each had a Datascriber hidden in the base of their landline telephones.

This real estate development was in a valley that had only one entrance. That roadway was monitored twenty-four hours a day. Grant Tillman ran the real estate office and only those passed by an ethereal board were allowed to buy.

At four o'clock each afternoon (Monday through Sunday) everyone but the rotating road sentry approached their flat tin-pan DS Machine and gathered with all the members of the Co-mind. Marchant Lewis took the head of the imagined Round Table and Lois Kim sat by his side. Other than this ceremonial structure, there was little of a recognizable hierarchy among the 120 humans and 31 animals that made up the future of mankind.

The first order of business was always each member reuniting with their cellular selves that had been distributed, growing the minds of others. The experience of life in this manner made every day nearly five months in duration. The separate selves had harrowing and transcendent experiences in the minds of coyotes, pigs, parrots, and other humans. Overnight people learned French or algebra or how to play chess. Humans experienced flight and animals saw patterns through human eyes that no philosopher would have ever imagined.

The Afternoon Merge included three people, along with Marchant Lewis, that had died within the past half year. These members showed no sign of waning and had chosen specific individuals in which they could store the sum total of their psychic experiences. It was decided early on that most animals and all children would be excluded from these meetings. Children because they could be molested and seduced so easily and animals because they died too soon and would ultimately overrun the population of the Co-mind if some limit were not placed upon them.

After the period in which individuals reunited with their other selves complaints of mistreatment were heard and some people were allowed to withdraw their presence in others' minds.

The final piece of business was the perpetual planning phase. This was where new members were suggested and new communities around the globe were planned. At these times Marchant would stand above the ethereal congress and exhort them about the new world he was hoping for. He was the mouthpiece of the Co-mind while Lois was the structure, but all the others were the flow of ideas and information and it was rare that anyone was chastised or punished. The nature of the Co-mind had to include the ideas of all its members.

Drunkenness and drug addiction were abolished naturally. Mental disease, even in the diagnosed mentally ill, was nonexistent.

For Lois the meetings were like the coming together of a great choir; or maybe a convocation of choirs that sang in different languages and were comprised of different species. Ideas moved like music and personalities like characters in an opera. There were no physical barriers to limit the range of expression. Men burst into flames, literally, expressing their love. Women grew into towering trees sheltering the ones that they lived for. Individuals became armies with a singular intention and beasts pondered great texts scrawled across the sides of mile-high cliffs.

And then there was the notion of time. There was no limit to space in the Co-mind and, contradictorily, no need for physical motion. In any afternoon meeting Lois had time enough to converse with everyone and all of her selves in the minds of everyone else.

Each night she made love at least a dozen times with various personages in the Co-mind. She flew with a thousand birds across vast bodies of water and climbed mountains with Strongbow, the resident ram. With some women she became a man for them, loved them, set up a home that either stayed or dissipated with the new meeting.

Kormok, the black bear, was maybe her best friend among all the residents of World's End. His senses were keen and his ideas cogent and broad. They spent what felt like years climbing the cold heights of the Sierra Nevada Mountains. She had never imagined such strength or tenderness. Some days they would lay in the sun taking in all the scents for miles around; Lana C darting around the outskirts, afraid to be too long in the presence of bears.

The Co-mind went on forever and the vestiges of individuals, it was postulated, could last for centuries; and each hundred years would be experienced as ten thousand. There was little conflict because the minds shared a space together. There was, as of yet, no Other, only being.

And together the members plotted a world where every adult and a member from every sentient species would be together without the false separations due to religions or genders, races or nationalities. World's End would put a stop to the strife and needless worries, the *reality* TV shows and the sexual frustrations, the prisoners and wardens of the world.

EARLY ONE THURSDAY morning Lois got in a car with Grant headed for San Francisco. They were to meet with Jenna Urdé at the prosecutor's office. Grant and Lois didn't talk much on the ride. They had drifted apart in the physical world. He had fallen in love with Cosette and Marie and they all lived together. Lois had regular conversations with Grant in her mind (and his) and she remembered these talks with a certain fondness but there was nothing to say on the long ride to the California coast.

THE STATE PROSECUTOR, Trent Cartwright, met with Lois and Jenna in a large corner office on the fourth floor of the justice building.

"You can be assured that we will convict you for one of these crimes, Ms. Kim," the heavyset and rubicund prosecutor promised.

"Grant Tillman says that it was a joke that got out of hand," Jenna Urdé said with little emphasis.

"What about Marchant Lewis?"

"He stipulated in his will that he wanted to be buried in the backyard. And your own coroner has ruled that he died from a massive heart attack occurring from natural causes."

"The burial was illegal," Trent said, grasping for some purchase. He was older, maybe sixty. Lois was thinking that a proficient and committed prosecutor would be good for the Co-mind in order to resolve disagreements among the fluid membership.

"Ms. Kim denies having anything to do with the burial. She's obviously too small to have done it in her own and you have no physical proof that she was involved."

This is the world we live in, Gooseberry, Marchant whispered in Lois's mind. *Justice based upon alienation and punishment. There is no search for truth or meaning. There is no desire for love.*

Do you love me, Marky? Lois inquired. Her mental tone was familiar and friendly.

You are my shelter from the storm of the world, my child, he replied. *I am because of you. All the others huddle together and fuck and talk but you are busy creating cities and populating them with magnificent beings both flawed and beautiful.*

Lois had used every free moment to create a vast metropolis named Antilla in the depths of her mind. There were millions there: humans and centaurs, metallic men and women and angels that had fallen from the uppermost reaches of Lois's mind. She seemed to be the only one who could create a lasting edifice other than the animals whose worlds were immense and immutable—permanent in a way that only instinct could inform.

Most of Lois's time was spent as the pedestrian queen of Antilla. She wandered the avenues talking to her subjects and leaving them to their own devices.

Most days she'd go to a small and shabby house in the middle of a large garden at the far western tip of the city. There Marchant Lewis lived. Instead of a desk he had a great, slowly rotating, globe floating before him. He studied the sphere making his plans for the domination of Earth. This small imagined house was the hub of the Co-mind, the center of the scheme to destroy the myths of man.

Many days Lois, the queen of Antilla, would sit next to Marchant, watching as he figured out how to get his agents into the religious, political, and criminal centers of the world. He would bring the edifices of mankind down around

their ears and then harness the genius of Earth to go out
beyond the stars.

I will need your help this afternoon, Lois thought.

*It is a mistake to take her. She is wrong. Something about
her tastes of metal, of something alien.*

I will do it without you, she told her mentor.

No, he said. *I will be there.*

"Are you listening to me, Ms. Kim?" Trent Cartwright
said.

"Can we leave now?" Lois asked Jenna.

"Certainly."

FIFTEEN

GRANT LEFT LOIS and Jenna to see his parents in Berkeley. He had wanted to admit his aging parents into the Co-mind but had so far been turned down by the group. It was likely that they would be allowed admittance when they came nearer to death but at this point they didn't have any evident talents that would benefit the Revolution of the Sublime.

Lois and Jenna went to a coffee shop near Fisherman's Wharf waiting for Grant to come.

"I don't think that Cartwright will try anything else," Jenna was saying. "His only hope is to get you to confess to something or to find new evidence. Stay out of his way and you won't have anything to worry about."

"Thank you," Lois replied gazing at the olive-eyed bar-rister. "I never doubted you."

Jenna hesitated, swiveled her head twenty degrees so that she was looking at Lois from the corner of her eye. "I've been meaning to ask you something."

"What?"

"When you and Grant, Mr. Tillman, talk to each other it seems like, like theres' some other conversation going on elsewhere, like you can read each other's thoughts. And he seems to defer to you even though we both know that kidnapping was for real."

Lois reached into her purse and came out with an aluminum tube that resembled an overly long and slender one-cigar humidor.

I have a bad feeling about her, Marchant Lewis whispered on a breeze. *She is not like anyone I have ever met. Not pliant like most minds.*

You don't know everything, Marky, Lois thought sharply.

But I know more about the subtleties of human nature than do you.

Ignoring the reprimand Lois addressed the lawyer. "Grant asked me to give you this."

Jenna looked at the tube for a moment, not reaching out. "What is it?" she asked.

"It contains the answer to your question."

Jenna took the tube and turned it around in her hands. "Where's the top?" she asked.

In answer Lois reached into her purse and grabbed an identical remote Datascriber that she had constructed with Marchant's help. This new version didn't need fiber optics; it instead used a modified short-wave signal that transferred data from one mind to the other.

The effect was instantaneous. The next thing Jenna knew she was sitting at a table in the center of a huge white room. The walls were so distant that they were hard to make out.

The floor could have well been infinite and empty white space. And sitting across from her was no longer the small and arrogant Asian woman but a humongous black man wearing an oversized purple jogging suit.

"What happened?"

"We are now of the mind, Jenna Urdé."

"Who are you?"

"Marchant Lewis."

Jenna looked closely at the man's face. It was similar to the photographs the prosecutor had submitted for evidence to the grand jury.

"You're dead."

"Yes," Lewis said, "in the corporeal sense. I have died but my mind lives on in Lois Kim's and, beyond that, in the vastness of the ever-growing Co-mind."

"Where is she?"

"She's watching."

When Marchant uttered these words Lois became aware of herself perceiving the white room and its inhabitants. Sometimes in her mind she found herself to be pure awareness without the distracting sense of self.

"What do you want?" Jenna asked. There was a smirk on her face.

Marchant frowned and Lois felt, for the first time what Marchant had been saying, that there was something different about Jenna—something wrong.

"We are the Co-mind," Marchant began.

"I understand," Jenna said, cutting him off. "You have found a way to bring minds together, to unify those that have lived in isolation and the tyranny of remote space."

Lois could see a transformation beginning in Jenna's form. This shouldn't be possible. A newly inducted member had never exhibited such power before. Jenna's form was turning semiopaque and amber. She rose in a flowing motion and Lois began a mad rush toward her.

Marchant found in himself the essence of the black bear Kormok and reared on his stout legs to meet the attack of Jenna's other, inner, self. But before the bear/man could move the amber creature struck.

Marchant/Kormok was down and the fluid hands of amber were constricting his throat. This was all symbol and metaphor but Lois knew that if she didn't act her friends would die. Somehow Jenna's hands had found all the cells in Lois's mind that held the memories and nature of Marchant and Kormok.

Lois buried both of her hands in the tacky fluid of Jenna's back and squeezed with a terrible strength born of the will for survival. At first this seemed to have no effect but then, after long moments of no-time, Jenna screamed and turned to Lois.

The face was extraordinary. It was crystalline and reddish, immobile and yet filled with the emotion of hatred.

"What are you?" Lois cried struggling to keep the monster's hands from her throat.

"I am stronger than you," the thing that was Jenna growled.

"What are you?"

"I am just born and older than the oldest edifice of man."

"What is your name?" Lois cried, begging and fighting for her life.

"Call me Urdé," the creature said. "The age of ice coming to drink the life from your marrow."

The creature called Urdé reached out for Lois but then somehow missed. Now that Lois, known in future generations as Lilith, knew the power of Jenna's hidden self she kept moving her focus from one *place* to another, avoiding the deadly grip of amber. She could see the bear Kormok running into the white distance.

"Who are you?" Lois screamed.

"I am Urdé," the creature said as she lunged again missing Lois by psychic inches. "I was born in the moment that you snared the fool woman into this place. I have been on this primitive rock for ten thousand thousand years moving from host to host without a mind or purpose. I am the seed of something your feeble minds could never imagine. We are here and you are soon to be forgotten."

Forgetting—the greatest threat to the Co-mind.

"Are you from Earth?" Lois Kim asked her mind expanding behind the blind of language.

"I am from the sky. I was the seed of a thought but now I am fully mindful. I will control every soul of every being in your world and we will go forth into realms that you poor, snuffling sacks of skin could never even imagine."

In the distance the white expanse was darkening.

"But why?" Lois asked, stalling, transforming.

"Why does the child crush a bug? Why does the beaver build his dams?" Urdé asked. "But more to the point why do you consume the flesh of life?"

There flashed through Lois's mind the image of billions of mindless human bodies staggering down alien streets,

building a great silver ark. Above this tableau was a plane
of pure thought where beings of infinite size dropped math-
ematical equations in various edible forms on planets
throughout the galaxy. In this plane, as in her mind, time
turned in on itself and extended. Ten million years was
nothing to these alien beings, these concepts. They would
have forgotten Jenna's psychic parasite but would welcome
it when it had taken over the Earth and brought its slaves
out into the void.

All life on Earth with flesh and mind would be enslaved
to Urdé.

The darkness was overcoming the light and Lois realized
that this might be the final metaphor of the Co-mind. She
leaped at Urdé and buried her hands deep into the thick
fluid flesh. She squeezed the alien psychic body with all her
might imagining death. But Urdé fought back covering Lois's ethereal body with her viscous liquid form.

The darkness in the distance was overcoming the light.
Lois felt the cold that Urdé promised seeping into her soul.
She renewed her battle against the alien being, the invader,
but she was aware that she didn't have the strength.

"Give up," Urdé whispered.

"Only in death," Lois hissed thinking, even at that semi-
nal moment, that the phrase was silly, overly dramatic.

"Your death will be my victory," Urdé said and the darkness rolled over them.

Lois girded her mind against Urdé intending to harm the
Other as much as possible before she was overcome. But
then she began to recognize images in the tumble of awareness that surrounded them. It was not her loss but Mar-

chant, embodied by Kormok, bringing all the members of the Co-mind and the fabricated citizens of Antilla to her aid.

Javier, wielding two machetes, was the first to attack Urdé. After that came Kormok, Andro the Mechanical Man, Windstar with her crystalline wings, and hundreds of others.

Urdé grew to the size of a six-story building but the members of the Co-mind and the rest of the beings of Lois's creation continued the attack.

Many were destroyed in their places in Lois's mind but they wore down the alien being, the Other, until she was the size and shape of a tennis ball. Just as Lois prepared to use her last bit of psychic energy to destroy the alien equation Marchant appeared before her.

"We cannot kill this being, Gooseberry."

"We must."

"No. We do not know if she was the only one among us. We have to study her, learn more about her origins and powers. We shall isolate her in a place in your mind where she cannot escape."

All around the city of Antilla was in ruin. Dead bodies were strewn about, destroyed by the surprise attack of the mind demon.

"What if she escapes?" Lois asked her eternal boarder.

"We must isolate ourselves from the Co-mind until we are certain that this cannot happen. We will communicate with them by letter and e-mail. We cannot chance even coming into proximity with them."

"So in the end it's just you and me here in this place that doesn't even exist," Lois said, not unhappily.

SIXTEEN

AND WITH THAT she opened her eyes. She was back at the table. It didn't surprise her that Jenna had fallen from her chair, onto the floor, dead. The seed called Urdé had grown to fully occupy Jenna's mind. It was not aware but it was everything inside her.

We have passed the first test toward world domination, Marchant whispered.

You are a monster, Lois responded as people all around ran to help the dead lawyer.

I am what I am, Marchant replied.

For some reason this soothed the young woman. She rose from her chair and walked out into the daylight planning even then the rebuilding of the world.